"What were you before?" Eden asked.

"What the Blackthorn men have been for hundreds of years," Nevada replied. "A warrior."

Vivid images from the fight in West Fork flashed before Eden's eyes, followed by other images. Nevada lying half-buried in rock with his rifle in his hand. Nevada checking the rifle firing mechanism with a few swift motions before he tried to stand up. Nevada's black eyes and unsmiling mouth.

Warrior.

It explained a lot. Too much.

The vivid joy that Eden had experienced moments before drained away, leaving sadness in its place. Her arms tightened protectively around Nevada's powerful body, as if she could somehow keep whatever might hurt him at bay. When she realized what she was doing, she didn't know whether to laugh or to weep at her own idiocy. Nevada needed protecting about as much as a bolt of lightning.

"For smoldering sensuality and exceptional storytelling, Elizabeth Lowell is incomparable."
—*Romantic Times*

ELIZABETH LOWELL

WARRIOR

MIRA BOOKS

ISBN 1-55166-032-6

WARRIOR

Copyright © 1991 by Two Of A Kind, Inc.

MIRA and the star colophon are trademarks of MIRA Books.

Printed in U.S.A.

for my editor, Pat Smith,
who knows that a hard man is good to find

MACKENZIE FAMILY: WESTERN LOVERS

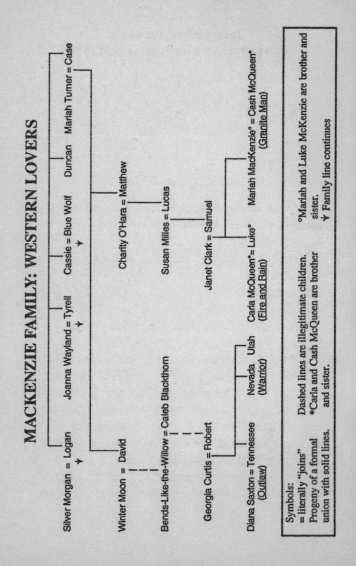

Symbols:
= literally "joins"

Progeny of a formal union with solid lines.

Dashed lines are illegitimate children.

*Carla and Cash McQueen are brother and sister.

°Mariah and Luke McKenzie are brother and sister.

↳ Family line continues

1

She's the wrong woman in the wrong place at the wrong time, Nevada Blackthorn thought, *and she's headed right for me.*

Nevada watched her approach in disbelief. Most people took one look at his light green eyes and unsmiling mouth and decided to strike up a conversation with someone else. Anyone else. This woman was different. She had taken one look at him and hadn't looked anywhere else.

With a grace that was totally unconscious, Eden Summers worked her way through the bar's crowded room, heading instinctively toward the dark, broad-shouldered man who sat alone. Very much alone. No one in the packed room came within arm's length of the man with the unflinching gaze and black, closely cut beard.

Even if she hadn't been told to "ask the guy with the beard" about supplies, Eden would have been drawn to this man. His isolation attracted rather than worried her. She was accustomed to working with solitary, wild animals.

"Hi, I'm Eden Summers," she said, smiling when she finally reached the bar. The lack of an answering smile didn't deter her. She would have felt better if she could have seen the color of his eyes, but they were shadowed by the brim of the black Stetson that he wore. "The man at the gas station said the store was closed, but that you might open it so I could buy supplies."

Eden's voice was like her smile, warm without being flirtatious. The tone was husky, as though she hadn't talked to anyone in hours. Nevada wondered if she would sound that way first thing in the morning, and if her taste would be half as sweet as her smile.

Even as he tried to push the sensual speculations aside, Nevada felt the rush of his body changing to meet the uncalculated femininity of Eden herself. It had been a long, long time since he had responded to a woman like that—quick and hot and hard, suddenly filled with a need as elemental as breathing itself.

"The man you're looking for is Bill," Nevada said, his voice roughened by the fierce racing of his blood. "He's the bartender."

"Oh. Sorry. Wrong beard." Eden's large hazel eyes went from Nevada's sleek, well-trimmed pelt to the bartender's rowdy chin fur. "That's Bill?"

Nevada nodded.

"Thanks," she said, smiling as she turned away.

Nevada nodded again and said nothing more. Nor did he smile. His bleak green glance went from Eden's lithe, alluring body to the faces of the men in West Fork's only bar. Every male in the packed, seething room had taken Eden's measure the instant she had come in the door. There was more than casual curiosity in their looks. Whether Eden knew it or not, the two other women present in the bar could most politely be described as working girls. Saturday in West Fork was their busiest time. They had been in and out of the bar and the adjoining motel with the regularity of clocks striking off the quarter hour.

When Eden turned away from Nevada, the men in the bar realized that she wasn't his date. Nor was there any other man hovering in the background, waiting for her. She was alone.

Instantly the men became more aggressive in their interest. In a town with one gas station, one general store, one café, one motel and one bar—all of which were collectively known as the OK Corral—strangers weren't that common. An unknown, attractive young woman with a graceful walk and a generous smile was unheard of.

And she had no man escorting her, no man to discourage the blunt sexual interest of the males in the bar.

Normally the lack of an escort wouldn't have been a problem for a woman, even in the wildest areas of the Four Corners Country of southwestern Colorado. But today wasn't normal. Today was West Fork's Eighth Annual Rattlesnake Roping Contest, an event that drew every bored, restless young man for a hundred miles around. As the snakes were still sleeping off winter—a fact that the men had counted on—approximately forty healthy males had spent the dreary March Saturday drinking beer, swapping lies and coarse jokes, ragging newcomers, passing comments about the availability and desirability of local females, playing practical jokes, and generally being a pain in the butt to everyone in the bar who wasn't at least four beers under the weather.

Nevada had been watching his second beer go flat and trying to decide which would be less tedious—helping the town's lone mechanic to patch a leaky gas tank on the Rocking M's pickup truck or watching the brawl that would inevitably break out in a bar jammed with bored young cowboys. On the whole, Nevada had been leaning toward patching leaky gas tanks when he had looked up and seen a flash of pale blond hair and the kind of easy-moving walk that was guaranteed to bring him to attention.

It had done the same for the other denizens of the OK Corral, who immediately assumed that the pretty stranger had come to West Fork for the kind of action that its bar was famous—or infamous— for delivering on a Saturday night.

Nevada knew that the other men's assumption was wrong. It wasn't just that Eden wore jeans, outdoor shoes and a hip-length down jacket. It was something both more subtle and more final than her lack of party clothes that told Nevada this woman was different. The openness and generosity in Eden's smile when she greeted him had announced that she wasn't in the market for sex. Women who were for sale were neither spontaneous nor uncalculating in their approach to life or men.

Unfortunately, Saturday in the bar at the OK Corral was the day and the place where pros and semipros came to display their shopworn wares. Eden's gentle manner and open smile didn't belong in the OK Corral's sexual marketplace, but she was there just the same.

Wrong place, wrong time, wrong woman.

And the longer she stayed there, the more insistent the men would become about attracting her attention.

With increasing irritation Nevada listened to the men nearby speculate on the subject of Eden's sexual expertise and price. He watched from the corner of his eye as the bartender came around the bar and stood close to Eden under the pretext that he couldn't hear her over the crude background comments. Standing that close wasn't necessary. Nevada, who was four feet away, could hear Eden all too well. She had a voice like summer, rich with warmth and life. The sensual promise in her voice made blood beat visibly at the base of Nevada's throat.

"The man at the filling station said you were closed, but that you might open the store so I could buy supplies," Eden said, speaking quickly, ignoring the catcalls and crass propositions coming from behind her. "There's no other store between here and the government cabin. I've driven all day, and there's supposed to be a storm in the high country tomorrow so I'll have to leave before dawn or take a chance on getting snowed out. As it is, I'll need a room for the night."

"No problem," Bill said, leaning back long enough to pull a room key from a board beneath the bar. He handed the key to Eden. "What else do you need?"

Before Eden could answer, a voice called out, "Yeah, that's it, Bill. Find out what she needs and I'll give it to her!"

Nevada didn't have to turn and look to know that the voice belonged to a young cowhand called Jones. Tall, well built and almost as handsome as he thought he was, Jones had earned his reputation as a lady-killer, drinker and fighter. Nevada's brother Tennessee had fired Jones from the Rocking M ranch. Since then, Jones had spent more time raising hell than working cattle. The cowboys drinking with Jones were the same as he was, too old to be boys and too undisciplined to be men.

Eden pocketed the key and acted as though she and the bartender were alone in the room.

"I need basics, mostly. Salt, sugar, flour, coffee—"

Jones inserted a stream of words that would have made a seasoned streetwalker wince. Nevada was the only man sober enough, and perceptive enough, to notice Eden's almost invisible flinching at the ugly language. But that was her only reaction.

"Hey, babe, look at me when I talk to you!" Jones yelled. "Pieces like you give me a pain. You sell it all over town and then act like you're a nun when a man tells you what he wants and how he wants it!"

Nevada's hand tightened on his beer bottle, a reflex as involuntary as his own arousal in Eden's presence. Slowly he relaxed his fingers.

Eden unzipped her jacket and pulled a small tablet from an inside pocket, praying that no one would notice the fine tremor of her fingers. She had dealt with too many wild animals not to have a sixth sense for danger. She was in danger now. What was a coarse verbal assault could change at any moment into something worse. The men around her had drunk enough to be uninhibited but not unable—and she was a stranger who had walked into their territory with nothing more to protect her than whatever basic goodness might exist beneath the veneer of civilization.

If the situation were different, Eden wouldn't have worried about being alone with even the cowboy who was running his mouth at her expense right now. But he had made his brags in front of the pack. Now he had to dominate her or lose face. It was an old, old story among animals.

And man was definitely an animal.

While Eden flipped through the tablet to find her supply list, Jones started wondering aloud what she would look like without her clothes, stripping her verbally, adding fuel to the savage fires that always burned just beneath the restraints of civilization.

Nevada turned and looked at Jones and the four men who were urging him on. The rest of the men in the room didn't notice Nevada's abruptly predatory intensity. They were watching Eden with the single-minded purpose of a pack of jackals closing in on their prey.

A glance at Eden told Nevada that she sensed the building ugliness. Beneath her calm expression was an animal wariness that increased with every deep voice that joined the chorus egging Jones on. Nevada had heard similar mutterings from men before, and with each guttural word civilization had been eroded a bit more until finally the savagery beneath broke free, destroying everything in its path that wasn't stronger and more vicious than itself.

With a feeling of acute relief, Eden found her supply list, tore it out, and handed it to the bartender. Not by so much as a fast sideways glance did she acknowledge that there was any other man in the room.

"This is all I need," she said.

Reluctantly Bill looked away from the opening in Eden's jacket to the piece of paper. He took it, scanned it quickly, and shrugged.

"Yeah, I got everything." His smile was just short of a leer as he looked back at Eden. "The store's in the next room. I'll unlock it for you. When you're done, holler and I'll open up the cash register."

"Thank you," Eden said, zipping her jacket again despite the stuffy heat of the bar. "I appreciate your kindness."

Bill had the grace to look uncomfortable.

With half-closed eyes, Nevada watched Eden follow the bartender through the inner door that joined the store and the bar. As though sensing that Nevada was watching, the bartender came back quickly and resumed selling drinks. The door joining the two rooms remained open. From where he sat at the bar, Nevada was in a position to watch both Eden and Jones without appearing to notice either one.

Through some eccentricity of the heating system, the empty store was even hotter than the crowded bar. Eden hesitated, then peeled off her stifling down jacket and worked quickly, finding supplies and stacking them on the checkout counter. When she was finished, she walked to the doorway. Backlit by the bright lights of the store, her distinctly feminine silhouette was a siren call far older than civilization.

A silence came over the bar.

"I'm ready, Bill."

Jones's hand shot out and fastened on the bartender's arm. "I'll take care of the little lady."

Jones grabbed his half-empty beer bottle and headed for the store. Four of his friends quickly followed. Although many of the men in the crowded bar looked around uneasily, no one stepped forward to stop Jones. Alone, the cowboy was bad enough. At the head of a pack, he was more trouble than anyone wanted to take on.

Except Nevada.

With a deceptively lazy motion Nevada came off the bar stool and stood between Jones and the path to Eden.

"Get out of my way," Jones said.

Nevada said nothing.

With a quick, practiced motion, Jones flicked his beer bottle against the side of the bar. The lower third of the bottle disintegrated, leaving behind the smooth neck and three wicked blades of glass.

Nevada neither moved nor spoke. He simply watched Jones and his four friends with the pale, unblinking green eyes of a cougar.

In the electric silence, Eden's harsh intake of breath was as clear as a scream. From her position in the doorway she could see that the dark, aloof stranger she had spoken to earlier was even more isolated now than he had been when she first walked into the barroom. She looked at Bill, who was backing away from the bar as quickly as he could, making clear that he wanted no part of whatever fight developed. The rest of the patrons obviously felt the same way. They were backing up as quickly as possible, leaving a wide clearing around the other men.

Alone, Nevada waited, feeling the world change as it always did when he was fighting, time stretching, dragging, nailed to the ground, leaving him free to move and other men mired in slow motion.

It was a primitive physiological gift, a trick of the adrenal glands, a quirk that had been passed down through centuries of Blackthorn warriors; adrenaline coursing through his body with each rapid heartbeat, speeding him up, a warrior's reflex that had saved Blackthorn lives when other, slower men had died.

Eden saw the subtle shifting of his body, the electric tension of a cougar set to spring.

"No!" Eden called, her voice tight with fear for him. "Damn it—no! There are five of them and you're not even armed!"

Having reached the same conclusion, Jones rushed forward, closing the distance between himself and Nevada.

Nevada moved.

His hands flashed out, grabbing Jones, then he pivoted, throwing him against the bar so hard that bottles danced and skidded. As Nevada finished the pivot, he smoothly converted his momentum into a different kind of force, lashing out with hands and feet in an intricate sequence. Two of Jones's buddies went to their knees and then onto their faces. One staggered backward and fell. The remaining cowboy grabbed one of his dazed friends, yanked him to his feet and headed for the exit.

Even though Eden was accustomed to seeing big cats take their prey, the speed, coordination and precision of Nevada's attack shocked her. He was so quick that individual motions blurred. Only the results were clearly visible. Three men down, two men running away.

Nevada's pale glance flicked over the remaining inhabitants of the bar, dismissed them as a source of danger, and came back to focus on Jones. With a silent, gliding stride, Nevada started forward to teach the cowboy the kind of lesson a man would be lucky to survive. But at the moment Nevada didn't really care about Jones's future. Better men had died and the world had kept on turning.

Just as Nevada reached for Jones, two slender, determined hands locked around one of Nevada's wrists. He could easily have shaken off the hands, but the combination of softness and strength was quintessentially feminine, disarming him. Eden smelled of sunshine and her breath was a rush of warmth flowing over him.

"Don't," Eden said softly, holding on to Nevada's hard arm, seeing his eyes for the first time. A cougar's eyes, pale green, bottomless, hell unleashed and waiting to spring. She brought his unresisting hand to her face. Her lips brushed his palm. "Please. He's not worth what it would cost you."

Eden felt the tiny shudder that ripped through Nevada's strength, sensed the gradual uncoiling of steel muscles, and breathed her thanks into his hard palm. Slowly her fingers slid from his arm until she no longer touched him.

Restrained by nothing more tangible than his acceptance of Eden's plea, Nevada reached once more for Jones. He lifted the heavy cowboy to his feet in a single motion. Stunned, Jones sagged between Nevada's hands.

"That's your free one," Nevada said calmly. "Understand?"

Jones tried to speak, couldn't, and nodded. Nevada opened his hands, releasing the cowboy. Jones staggered, caught himself on a bystander, then pushed free and reeled toward the front door. He didn't even pause to look at the two groaning men who had followed him into the fight.

"Take them with you," Nevada said.

His voice was still soft, but it carried clearly through the stunned silence of the room. Struggling, limping, able to use only one arm, Jones got the two other men upright and out the door.

Nevada turned to the bartender. "Total her bill."

"Sure thing, Nevada," the man said hastily. "Right away."

His hurried footsteps were the only sound in the bar. Nevada turned and looked at each man in the room as the tense silence stretched. Smoothly he stepped behind Eden, putting his hands on her shoulders.

"Gentlemen," Nevada said softly, his tone transforming the word into an insult, "I want you to meet Eden Summers. In the future you will treat her the same as you would Carla, Diana, Mariah or any other Rocking M woman."

Nevada said no more. He didn't have to.

"Go get your supplies," Nevada said, squeezing Eden's shoulders reassuringly before he released her.

While Eden paid her bill, Nevada shrugged into his shearling jacket, leaned casually against the bar and waited for the groceries to be bagged.

Slowly the other men in the bar turned away and began talking in subdued voices. Most of the conversations centered around the fight. Or rather, around Nevada. Tennessee Blackthorn's lethal fighting skills were well-known. Nevada's had often been speculated upon, but no one had been curious enough to rattle his cage and find out for sure.

Until tonight. West Fork had just discovered that the aloof, silent cowhand called Nevada was every bit as skilled at fighting as he was at tracking cougars—and he was known as the best cat-tracker in five states.

When Eden was ready, Nevada helped her carry the supplies. Outside a raw March wind combed the streets, sending shivers of motion over puddles that had just begun to freeze in the early evening chill. Where there was no snow, the landscape had taken on a vague hint of green, promise of the hot summer to come. For now, it was promise only. The earth itself was still locked within winter's cold.

In the distance an isolated group of mountains rose against the darkening sky. Clouds gathered and slowly seethed around the peaks. Other clouds stretched in a wind-smoothed front across the icy arch of the sky. Eden glanced overhead, saw the weather front that was supposed to bring snow, and debated whether or not to take on the rough road between West Fork and the government cabin that would be her home until June.

"You'll be safe enough at the motel," Nevada said, following Eden's glance at the weather front. "No one will bother you now."

The subtle rasp in Nevada's deep voice intrigued Eden. But then, everything about him intrigued her, and had from the first instant she had seen him.

"Thank you," she said quietly. "If I had known what West Fork was like, I would have bought my supplies in Cortez."

Nevada shrugged. "Most of the time West Fork is real quiet. You just came on the one Saturday a year when the local half-wits get together and howl. Two hours earlier and no one would have been drunk enough to run off at the mouth. Two hours later and they would have been too drunk to care who came through the door."

"I doubt that you ever get that drunk," Eden said matter-of-factly. She braced a sack of supplies on her hip as she unlocked the truck's door. "You're too disciplined."

Nevada gave Eden a sharp look, but before he could ask her how she had known that about him, he saw a huge, dark shadow moving inside the cab of the weather-beaten truck.

"Good God—is that a wolf?" Nevada demanded.

Eden smiled. "You're mostly right. The rest is husky." The truck's door grated as it opened. "Hello, Baby. You ready to stretch your legs a bit?"

A black tail waved and sounds of greeting that were a cross between a growl and a muffled yip came from the wolf's thickly furred throat. The instant Nevada moved toward the truck, the sounds became a definite growl and the tail ceased waving.

"It's all right, Baby. Nevada is a friend."

The growls ended. Yellow eyes looked at Nevada for a comprehensive instant. Then, accepting the stranger, Baby leaped to the ground.

"Baby?" Nevada asked dryly. "He's got to go at least a hundred and twenty pounds."

"One hundred and thirty-three. But he started small. I found him in a hunter's trap when he was half-grown. The leg healed almost as good as new, but not quite. In the wild, the difference would have slowly killed him.''

''So you kept him.''

Eden made a murmurous sound of agreement as she leaned into the passenger side of the truck to deposit supplies.

''Do you make a habit of collecting and taming wild animals?''

''No.'' Eden stacked two sacks where a passenger's feet would have gone. ''I'm a wildlife biologist, not a zookeeper. If I find wild animals that are hurt, I heal them and turn them loose again. If I kept them, there's nothing I could give them that would compensate for the loss of their freedom.''

Silently Nevada handed over the sacks he was carrying. As he did, Eden noticed that he had cut his left hand in the fight. She dumped the sacks in the truck and took Nevada's hand between her own.

''You're hurt!''

Nevada looked down into Eden's eyes. In the fading light of day her eyes were almost green, almost gold, almost amber, almost blue gray, a shimmer of colors watching him, as though every season, every time, lived behind her eyes. Her hands on his skin had the healing warmth of summer, the softness of spring sunshine. He wanted nothing more than to bend down and take her mouth, her body, sinking into her until he couldn't remember what it was like to be cold.

But that would only make the inevitable return of ice all the more painful.

"I'm fine," he said, removing his hand.

Eden took Nevada's hand again. The renewed touch of her skin sent hunger searching through every bit of his big body, making his muscles clench with need.

"Nevada," she said, remembering what the bartender had called him. "That's your name, isn't it?"

Nevada nodded curtly, trying to ignore the exquisite heat of Eden's breath as she examined his hand again.

"You're bleeding, Nevada. Come with me to the motel room. I'll clean the cut and—"

"No."

His rough refusal surprised her. She looked up into eyes as cold and bleak as a winter moon.

"It's the least I can do to thank you for being a gentleman," Eden said softly.

"Take me to your motel room?" Nevada asked, his tone sardonic.

"You know that isn't what I meant."

"Yes. But I mean it." Nevada freed his left hand, hesitated, then let out his breath with a whispered curse. His fingertip skimmed the curve of Eden's lower lip with aching slowness. "Stay away from me, Eden. I'm a warrior, not a knight in shining armor, and I want you more than all the men in that bar put together.''

Abruptly Nevada turned and walked away, leaving Eden standing motionless in the icy twilight, watching him with a mixture of shock and deeply sensual speculation in her eyes.

2

The big Appaloosa threw up its head and snorted.

"Take it easy, you knothead," Nevada said soothingly. Then, without turning around, he added, "'Morning, Ten. Hear anything from Mariah and Cash?"

Tennessee Blackthorn was accustomed to his brother's uncanny ability to tell when he was being approached from behind, and by whom. Even so, Ten had hoped that after almost two years on the Rocking M, Nevada would lose some of the habits of a guerrilla warrior. But he hadn't. He had the same fighting edge to his reflexes and senses that he had had in the mountains of Afghanistan, where he had taught warriors with flintlocks how to defeat soldiers with tanks. Nevada had the same intense discipline and concerted lack of emotion that he had learned in Afghanistan. Even the Rocking M's cowhands had given up betting on when—or under what circumstances—Nevada Blackthorn would truly smile.

"Cash called late yesterday," Ten said. "Mariah's doctor said she was fine. Apparently she missed the flu that was going around here."

"Good."

"Speaking of being sick, are you sure you should be on your feet? That was a fair fever you were running yesterday."

"I'm glad Mariah isn't sick," Nevada said, settling the saddle gently over the skittish Appaloosa. "She and Cash should have fine, strapping children. I'm looking forward to hearing another healthy baby around here hollering for mama to bring his next meal. Carla's new baby is really something." Nevada cinched up the saddle girth with a swift, smooth motion, moving so quickly that the horse had no time to object. "Like your Carolina. That's one fine set of lungs the little lady has. She and Logan make a real pair."

Ten smiled dryly and accepted that Nevada wasn't going to talk about flu, rest, and a cold ride into the mountains. "Glad you like having babies around. Mariah will give us two more little screamers sometime in May or June."

Nevada looked over his shoulder. "Twins?"

"Yeah. Cash was so excited he could hardly talk. He and Mariah had been hoping, but they hadn't said anything until they were sure everything was fine."

"Tell her to be extra careful. Twins tend to be born small, and small babies have a harder time."

"Tell her yourself. She'll be here tomorrow."

"I won't." Nevada gestured with his head toward MacKenzie Ridge. "I'm going to spend a few days tracking cats. Supposed to be fresh snow by afternoon up toward Wildfire Canyon. It may be the last tracking snow of the winter."

And maybe, just maybe, when I'm chasing cats rather than fighting fever dreams, I'll be able to see something other than extraordinary hazel eyes and a warm mouth that trembles at the lightest touch of a man's finger.

The back door of the ranch house slammed as someone left the dining room. The Appaloosa shied wildly. Nevada cursed in the silence of his mind and brought his attention back to the horse.

"I can see why Luke gelded that one," Ten muttered. "Target has more brains in his spotted butt than between his ears."

Nevada shrugged. "As long as you pay attention, he's the best winter horse on the Rocking M." With the unconscious ease of a man performing a familiar task, Nevada gathered the roping rein, stepped into the stirrup and mounted in a single easy motion. "Especially in fresh snow. Target's big enough not to get bogged down in the drifts."

"Wouldn't life be simpler if you just shot the cougars with a tranquilizer dart, put a radio collar on them and tracked them from the air?"

"Simpler? Maybe. A hell of a lot more expensive for sure. And a hell of a lot less fun for the cats—and me."

Ten laughed softly. "That's what Luke said. I didn't argue." Ten started to turn away, then remembered something else. "You know that old cabin just beyond Wildfire Canyon?"

"The one at the end of that abandoned logging road?"

Ten nodded. "A guy from the government called yesterday to tell us that some cougar specialist will be using the cabin as a base camp for the next month or two, depending on the cats. So if you find signs of someone moving around in the high country, don't worry. Luke and I agreed to give free access to Rocking M land as long as we got a copy of whatever report is filed about the cougars."

At the word *cabin*, Nevada went very still. A conversation that was three days old echoed in his mind.

There's no other store between here and the government cabin.

"Did anyone mention the name of the cat expert?" Nevada asked.

"I don't think so. Why?"

For a moment Nevada said nothing, remembering Eden's gentle voice and surprisingly strong hands, and the utter lack of fear in her eyes when she had seen the elemental violence in his.

Do you make a habit of collecting and taming wild animals?

No. I'm a wildlife biologist, not a zookeeper.

Eden's voice, her scent, the tactile memory of her alluring warmth...they had haunted Nevada's waking hours. They might have haunted his sleep as well, but he would never know. It was a pact he had made with himself years ago. He never remembered dreams.

"There was a young woman in West Fork last Saturday," Nevada said evenly. "She said something about being a wildlife expert."

"Last Saturday?" Ten said, his gray eyes narrowing.

Though Nevada had said nothing, word of the fight had gone through the Four Corners area of Colorado like forked lightning.

Nevada nodded.

"A woman, huh?"

Nevada nodded again.

"Pretty?" Ten asked, his handsome face expressionless.

"Why? You getting tired of Diana?"

The idea was so ridiculous that Ten laughed aloud. Then his smile vanished and he looked every bit as hard as his younger brother.

"The next time you go one on five," Ten said, "I'd take it as a personal favor if you'd let me guard your back. Luke made the same offer. So did Cash."

The left corner of Nevada's mouth turned up very slightly, as close as he ever came to a smile. "Cash, too, huh? Does that mean he's finally forgiven me for noticing that Mariah was pregnant before he did?"

"When a man is unsure of a woman, he's apt to be a bit blind," Ten said in a bland voice.

"He's apt to be a horse's butt."

"Your turn will come."

"Yours sure did," Nevada retorted, remembering the tense months before Ten had finally admitted that he was irrevocably bound to Diana. "I'll tell you, Tennessee, if I never tangle with you again, it will be too soon."

"Yeah, well, the hands are taking bets on that one too, especially since word got out that Utah's coming back as soon as he gets out of the hospital. Guess he's finally gotten his fill of jungle fighting."

"At least they don't need to worry about Utah getting in a brawl over a woman. Not since Sybil." Nevada leaned forward in the saddle. A flick of his hand freed the packhorse's lead rope from the corral railing. "The real shame about Sybil is that she wasn't a man," Nevada continued, reining Target toward the mountains. "If she were a man, I'd have killed her."

Before Ten could speak, Nevada kicked the big Appaloosa. "Shake a leg, Target. We've got a long ride ahead."

Even with the eager, powerful Appaloosa beneath him, it was afternoon before Nevada rode into Wildfire Canyon's wide mouth. In all but the worst winter storms, the canyon's alignment with the prevailing winds kept the flat floor swept relatively free of snow. Patches of evergreens clothed the sloping sides of the canyon, tall trees whose ages were almost all the same. The fire that had given the canyon its name had swept through eighty years before, burning the living forest to ash, leaving behind a ghost forest of heat-hardened skeletons. A few of those skeletons still stood upright amid the new forest, their weather-smoothed shapes silver and black in the full sun or moonlight.

The on-again, off-again warmth of March had melted the snow in places, revealing dark ground. Snowdrifts remained in narrow gullies and ravines, and beneath the most dense forest cover. Yet even in the higher altitudes, winter was slowly losing its white grip on the land. Water sparkled and glittered everywhere, testimony to melting snow. Drops gathered into tiny rivulets, joined in thin streams, merged into small, rushing creeks. Today the drops would freeze again, but only for a short time. Soon they would be free to run down to the distant sea once more.

Soon, but not yet. The storm that had threatened three days before hadn't materialized. It was coming now, though. As Target followed the zigzagging trail that led out of the northern end of Wildfire Canyon, Nevada could smell the storm on the wind, feel it in the icy fingers ruffling his beard and making his eyes sting. Even the rocks around him weren't impervious. They had known the grip of countless winters, water silently freezing, expanding, splitting stones apart. Evidence of the silent, inexorable power of ice lay everywhere in the high reaches of the canyon, where slopes too steep to grow trees were covered with angular stones that had been chiseled from boulders and bedrock by countless picks of ice.

At the top of the steep trail, Nevada reined in and let Target rest for a few minutes. Between gusts of wind, the silence was complete. The tiniest sound came clearly through the air—a pebble rolling from beneath steel-shod hooves, a raven calling across the canyon. Target's ears flicked and twitched nervously as he tried to hear every sound. When a pebble dislodged by water clattered down the slope, the horse's nostrils flared, the skin on his shoulder flinched and he shied.

"Take it easy, boy," Nevada said in a soothing voice as he gathered in the roping rein more tightly.

Even as Nevada's left hand managed the reins, his right hand checked that the rifle was still in its saddle holster. The gesture was so automatic that he was unaware of it, legacy of commando training and years spent in places where to be unarmed was to die. The rifle's cold, smooth stock came easily into his hand, then settled back into the sheath.

Target snorted and bunched his haunches, wanting to be free of the pressure of the bit. Nevada glanced at the packhorse. Daisy was ignoring Target's nervousness.

"Settle down, knothead," Nevada said calmly. "If there was anything around but wind and shadows, Daisy would know it. She has a nose like a hound."

Target chewed resentfully on the bit as the wind gusted suddenly, raking the landscape with fingernails of ice. Nevada tugged his hat down more firmly and guided the horse out onto the exposed slope. For the first hundred yards, a faint, ragged line across the wind-scoured scree was the only sign of a trail. The line had been left by generations of deer, cougars, and occasional Indians. In modern times, deer and cougars still used the game trail, as did Rocking M cowhands who were working both

Wildfire Canyon and the leased grazing lands beyond.

Target was in the center of the scree when the black flash of a raven skimming over the land spooked him. Between one heartbeat and the next, Target tried to leap over his own shadow.

There was no time for Nevada to think, to plan, to escape. Reflex took over. Even as Target lost his footing on the loose stone, Nevada was kicking free of the stirrups, grabbing the rifle, and throwing himself toward the uphill side of the trail. Inches away from his rider's body, Target's powerful hooves flailed as the horse lost its balance and began rolling down the slope in a clattering shower of loose stone. Nevada fell too, turning and rolling rapidly, surrounded by loose rocks, no way to stop himself, nothing solid to hang on to.

At the bottom of the slope, a massive boulder stopped Nevada's body. Before the last stone in the small landslide had stopped rolling, Target staggered to his feet, shook himself thoroughly, and looked around. When nothing happened, the horse walked calmly to the edge of the recent slide and looked for something edible. A few minutes later the packhorse joined Target, having found a less dangerous way to the bottom of the slope.

Before long the gray sky lowered and dissolved into the pale dance of countless snowflakes. The horses turned their tails to the wind and drifted before the storm.

Nevada lay unmoving, rifle in hand.

Baby's ululating howl brought Eden to her feet in a rush of adrenaline. The wolf had been running free all day, for Eden hadn't yet needed Baby's keen nose. She would put him to work after the storm had passed, leaving a fragile shawl of white over the land. Then she would roam widely, noting and recording the cat tracks that would show clearly in the fresh snow. Once the snow melted away, Baby's nose would make certain that Eden could follow the cats even across solid rock.

A steaming cup of coffee in her hand, Eden went to the cabin door, opened it and listened. The slow glide of snowflakes to the ground and muffled sounds limited visibility to a hundred feet.

Baby howled again, calling out in the eerie harmonics of his wolf father.

Eden listened closely and muttered, "Not his hunting song. Not his lonely song. Not his great-to-be-alive song."

The haunting cry rose again, closer now, piercing the snow's silence.

"I hear you, Baby. You're coming back to me."

A black shape materialized at the edge of the snowfall. With the ghostly silence of smoke, Baby came across the meadow clearing to the cabin.

There was a brief hesitation in his gait, a slight asymmetry in his stride, which was the legacy of the steel trap that had maimed him years before.

Instead of greeting Eden and going about his business, Baby caught her hand delicately in his mouth and looked at her with intent yellow eyes. Curiosity leaped in Eden. Baby rarely insisted on having her attention. When he did, it was to warn her that they weren't alone any longer—men were somewhere near.

"Company is coming, hmm?" After what had happened in West Fork, Eden was glad for the presence of the huge, dark wolf. "Well, don't worry. I just made a big pot of coffee. Come on in, Baby. We'll greet whoever it is together."

Eden tried to withdraw her hand. Politely, gently, Baby's jaws tightened.

Curiosity gave way to a fresh rush of adrenaline in Eden. A picture condensed in her mind—eyes of pale icy green, a thick black pelt of hair and beard, a face that was too hard to be called handsome and too fiercely good-looking to be called anything else.

Stay away from me, Eden.... I want you more than all the men in that bar put together.

It was not the first time Eden had thought of the dark stranger who had come to her aid. His image condensed between her eyes and the hearth fire, the wild sky, the rugged land. He haunted her with questions that couldn't be answered.

Who are you, Nevada? Where are you? Is it your scent on the snow-wind that is calling to my wolf?

As soon as the hopeful thought came, Eden pushed it aside. Nevada hadn't looked back after he had walked away from her. He hadn't left any message for her the following morning. He hadn't even told her his last name.

Eden looked into Baby's eyes and wished futilely that she could truly communicate with him. Baby had been this insistent only once before, in Alaska, when it was a silvertip grizzly sniffing around downwind rather than a lonely trapper smelling smoke and hoping for a cup of fresh coffee.

"Are you sure it's important, Baby? Mortimer J. Martin, Ph.D., personally assured me there were no bears left in this part of the Lower Forty-eight. That's why I left my rifle with Dad."

Baby made a soft, somehow urgent sound deep in his throat and tugged on Eden's hand. Then he released her, trotted away about twenty feet and looked over his shoulder.

"You're sure? Compared to the Yukon there isn't enough snow to mention, but I'm really not dying for a hike in the white stuff. There's not enough snowpack for cross-country skis or snowshoes, which means—"

Baby whined softly, pleading in the only way he could. Then he threw back his head and howled.

The hair on the back of Eden's neck stirred in primal response. Not even for the grizzly had Baby been so insistent.

"Baby, *stay.*"

Knowing without looking that the wolf would obey, Eden spun around and ran back into the cabin. She grabbed a canteen, filled it with hot coffee, banked the hearth fire, yanked on two layers of snow gear, shrugged into the backpack she always kept ready to go and ran out the front door in less than three minutes. She glanced at her watch, wondering how long she would be gone. If necessary she could live out of her backpack for several days. She would just as soon have the comforts of the cabin, however.

"Okay, Baby. Let's go."

The wolf didn't waste any time. He set off at a purposeful trot across the meadow through the evergreens. Eden walked swiftly behind, pacing herself so that she would neither tire quickly nor become sweaty. Sweat was one of the greatest hazards of snow country, for when a person stopped moving, sweat froze, creating a layer of ice against the skin that sapped warmth dangerously.

Baby was careful never to get out of Eden's sight. Nor did he run with his nose to the ground as though following a trail. Gradually Eden realized that Baby was retracing his own steps—in places where snow had gathered, his tracks went in both directions.

Eden had been following Baby for ten minutes when she saw the first hoofprints in a patch of snow. Two horses, one with a rein or a rope dragging. They were headed roughly southeast and she was headed roughly north. Baby ignored the horse sign even though Eden could see it was very fresh. The softly falling snow hadn't yet blurred the crisp edges of the tracks. She stopped, stared off through the snow and thought she saw a vague shape that could have been a horse standing in the shelter of a big evergreen.

"Baby!"

The wolf stopped, gave a short, sharp bark and resumed trotting.

After only an instant of hesitation, Eden kept on following Baby. She would trust the half-wild, half-tame animal's uncanny instincts. If Baby wasn't interested in the horse it was because he had more important game in mind.

Without turning aside even once, Baby retraced his own tracks. The forest ended at the foot of a scree slope. Automatically Eden checked the barren slope first. Even beneath the veil of falling snow, the story of what had happened was clear: at least one horse had come skidding and rolling down through the scree, starting a small rockslide in the process. Hoofprints led away from the disturbed ground. There was no sign of any horse nearby.

Baby never hesitated. He darted over the loose debris left by the slide and sat near a massive boulder ten yards from Eden. There the slide had parted like water, leaving behind larger rocks before closing around the downhill side of the car-size boulder.

"Baby? What—"

Eden's breath broke, then came in harshly as she realized that something lay half-buried in the loose stone that had piled against the huge boulder.

A man.

His body blended with the rubble from the recent slide. Fresh snowfall was rapidly blurring all distinctions between stone and flesh. The man was motionless, yet hauntingly familiar. His bearded face was turned up to the chill softness of falling snow.

"Nevada!"

No motion answered Eden's cry.

3

$\sim\!\!\infty\!\!\sim\!\!\infty\!\!\sim$

Eden scrambled through the loose debris and threw herself down at Nevada's side. Even as she ripped off her gloves and felt for his pulse, she saw the brassy glitter of spent shell casings scattered on top of the rocky rubble. A rifle was still gripped in Nevada's big right hand. The skin of his left wrist was cool but not chilled. He must have been conscious at some time since his fall, for he had fired the rifle repeatedly.

"Nevada," Eden said, pitching her voice to be both reassuring and distinct. Still talking, she moved back from him so that she could shrug out of her backpack and down jacket. "Nevada, can you hear me?"

A shudder rippled through his powerful body. His eyes opened, a cougar's eyes, trapped, dangerous. The fingers holding the rifle tightened. Eden didn't notice, for she was spreading her bright red jacket over his chest.

"Do you hurt anywhere?" she asked.

When Nevada's eyes focused on her, they changed. Life and light came back into them. He shook his head as though to clear it.

"If you can do that, you didn't break your neck."

Relief was bright in Eden's voice. Growing up on a homestead in Alaska had taught her the basics of first aid—splinting breaks, stitching up gashes, and the dangers of hypothermia, but spine injuries were beyond her skills.

And the thought of Nevada hurt bothered Eden deeply.

She pulled off the knitted ski hat she had worn underneath her jacket hood. A moment later she was leaning over Nevada, stretching the hat to cover Nevada's short black hair, tucking stray strands in, her face only inches from his, her breath bathing his cheeks above his beard, her soft hair touching him when she turned her head.

"There. That will help you to stay warm."

"Eden? What the hell are you doing out here?"

"Ask Baby. He dragged me out of a nice warm cabin and insisted I go for a walk in the snow."

Gently Eden lowered Nevada's head back to the ground, cushioned the rocks beneath with one of her jacket's quilted sleeves, and looked closely at

Nevada's pale green eyes. Both pupils were the same size and he was studying her with an intensity that was almost tangible. Whatever else had happened in his fall, his faculties were intact.

"Thank God," Eden said too softly for Nevada to hear.

But he did, just as he felt the rushing warmth of the sigh she gave, as though the weight of the mountainside had just slipped from her shoulders.

"Baby must have found you earlier, sensed something was wrong and came back to get me," Eden continued, tucking her bright jacket around Nevada's broad chest.

Nevada blinked, scattering snowflakes that had tangled in his thick black eyelashes. "Be damned. Thought I saw a wolf a while back, but there aren't any wolves around here, so I chalked it up to taking a header down the mountain."

"You did that, all right. Where do you hurt?"

"Nowhere."

Eden looked skeptical. "Then why are you lying here?"

"My left foot is wedged against the big boulder. When I couldn't dig myself out, I began firing my rifle three rounds at a time."

Eden nodded. Three spaced shots were a universal come-running signal. "Baby must have heard the shots or caught your scent on the wind." She turned back to the knapsack, pulled out the canteen, and took off the top. The coffee was still hot. She put the canteen in Nevada's hands. "This will help to warm you. Drink as much as you can while I look at your foot."

Nevada inhaled deeply. "Damn. That smells like real coffee."

"Guaranteed strong enough to grow hair on the bottom of your feet," Eden agreed as she began pulling on her gloves.

The corner of Nevada's mouth shifted unnoticeably beneath his beard as he lifted the canteen and drank deeply. The hot, rich liquid spread through his body like a benediction, warming everything it touched. Reluctantly he stopped drinking.

"You want some?" he asked.

"I'm plenty warm," Eden said. "Drink as much as you can hold."

"That will be all of it."

"Good."

While Nevada finished the coffee, Eden began pushing loose rock away from his hips and legs, clearing a way to the trapped ankle. As she worked, she tried not to notice the clean, powerful lines of his body. It was impossible. He was a large, healthy male animal, and he called to her senses in ways that disconcerted her.

Nevada licked the last drop of coffee from his mustache and watched Eden working over his legs. Her motions were sure, efficient and productive.

Obviously she wasn't going to come apart in an emergency.

He liked that as much as he liked the breasts swaying beneath her ski jersey and pullover sweater and the decidedly female curves of her hips. But admiring Eden's body was having a pronounced effect his own, so he concentrated on her face instead, memorizing the smooth skin of her cheeks, the changing colors of her hazel eyes, the tempting sweetness of her mouth.

Eden looked up, sensing Nevada's intense regard. He shifted his glance to the slope.

"You see any horses on the way here?" he asked.

"Just tracks. A big horse and a smaller one. Both are wearing winter shoes. Both are drifting south and east in front of the wind." Stones clattered and rattled, pushed by Eden's hands as she resumed digging. "I might have seen one of them under a big evergreen about five minutes up the trail, but I couldn't be sure. The smaller horse is dragging a rope or a rein. Neither of the horses is limping, although the bigger one rolled down the same slope you did. If there was any blood, it wasn't much. So relax. Your horses are better off than you are."

"Big horse. Small horse. Winter shoes. Rope." Nevada looked at Eden's clean profile and asked neutrally, "Where did you learn how to track?"

"Alaska."

"Horses?" he asked skeptically.

"Cats," Eden said, struggling to shove aside a rock that was smaller than a pony, but not much. "I studied lynx in the north woods. I came to Colorado to study cougars. After cats, tracking horses is a piece of cake."

Nevada's eyes changed, intensity returning. Eden was going to be living in the remote area around Wildfire Canyon, tracking the cougars that had returned to the Rocking M.

And so was he.

"Damn," Eden said under her breath. She braced her shoulder and tried again to shift the smaller of the two boulders that had trapped Nevada's foot. "Did you try pulling your foot out of your boot?"

"Yes. Rest before you start sweating."

She hesitated, then nodded. He was right. She sat back on her heels and breathed deeply, trying not to let her worry show. Nevada's left foot was securely wedged between a rock that was too big for her to shift and the massive boulder that had broken the back of the landslide. Loose rubble slithered and stirred and eased downhill every time she tried to dig him out.

"How's your head?" As Eden asked the question, her eyes were searching the slope for something to use as a lever against the smaller of the two boulders that were holding Nevada captive.

"I'll live."

"Dizzy? Double vision? Nausea?"

"No. I have a hard skull."

She smiled without looking at him, still searching for a lever. "I won't touch that line. How bad is your foot?"

"Cold is a good anesthetic."

"Too good. You were unconscious when I got here."

"I would have awakened in ten minutes and fired three more rounds."

Nevada's certainty made Eden look back at him.

"Hypothermia—" she began.

"It's not a problem yet," he interrupted flatly. "I've been a lot colder under a lot worse conditions and functioned just fine."

Eden tugged off one glove, grabbed Nevada's wrist and started counting. His pulse was strong. Cold hadn't slowed his body processes yet. And the quart of hot coffee would help hold the chill of the ground at bay.

"All right." Unconsciously Eden caressed Nevada's left wrist and his palm with her fingertips, reassured by his tangible heat and the resilience of his flesh. Like Baby, Nevada fairly radiated an elemental vitality. "Where did you learn to sleep and wake yourself whenever you wanted?"

"Afghanistan." His voice was clipped, foreclosing any other questions.

"They have some big mountains there, and a lot of mines," Eden said absently. She looked past him to the forest, focusing on a piece of deadfall that might work as a lever. "Are you a geologist?"

"No."

Despite the warning in Nevada's voice, Eden was beginning to ask another question when she felt wetness on her fingertips. She looked down and saw a trickle of blood across Nevada's hand. Ignoring his brief protest, she eased off his leather glove. A jagged, partially healed cut went across the back of his hand. The scab had been broken in one place. Fresh blood oozed slowly toward his tanned wrist.

Eden breathed Nevada's name and stroked the uninjured flesh on either side of the cut. Memories of anger and fear and the razor edges of a freshly broken beer bottle lanced through her.

"You should have let me take care of you," she said quietly.

"I don't need a woman to take care of me. I never have. I never will."

This time the warning in Nevada's voice got through.

"Really?" Eden asked casually. "Then I hope you're comfortable, cowboy. It may be a long time before a *man* comes along this particular piece of mountainside."

There was a tight silence before the left corner of Nevada's mouth shifted very slightly.

"You must be the exception that proves the rule," he said.

"Gosh, I'm so glad you explained that to me. I was beginning to wonder if you hadn't hit your head too hard on one of those rocks."

Suddenly Eden frowned and shifted her grip on Nevada's wrist. "Are you sure you feel all right? Your pulse is pretty fast right now."

"My resting pulse is in the low sixties."

"But—"

"I'm not resting."

"You have a point. But your pulse has increased in the past minute or two."

"If a man were leaning over me and stroking my wrist like a lover, my pulse wouldn't have budged."

It took a few moments for the meaning of Nevada's words to get past Eden's concern for him. A rising tide of color marked the exact instant of her understanding that she was cradling his hand between her own. Even worse, she was running her fingertips caressingly from the pulse point on his wrist to the base of his fingers and back again.

"Sorry," Eden said, dropping Nevada's hand. She pulled on her glove again and she spoke quickly. "I'm a tactile kind of person. When I'm nervous or worried or thinking hard, I tend to stroke things. You were within reach."

It was partly true. The rest of the truth was that there was something about Nevada Blackthorn that made Eden want to stroke him, to learn his textures and pleasures, to make him smile, to warm him, to... heal him.

And then set him free?

There was no answer except Eden's silent, inner cry of pain at the thought of Nevada turning away from her again. The depth of her reaction was irrational, and she knew it. She also knew it was as deep as a night sky, and as real. Knowing that, she stopped fighting her response to Nevada. Working in the wild as much as she did had taught her to accept things that did not make sense within the narrow cultural limits of modern rationality.

"Tactile, huh?" Nevada drawled. "Must make life interesting for the men around you."

"The only men in my life have fur and fangs and go on all fours."

Stones rattled as Eden went back to work clearing debris around Nevada's trapped ankle. It seemed that for every two handfuls she pushed aside, a handful more slithered down to fill the depression.

"Can you reach my backpack?" Eden asked after a few minutes.

Instead of answering, Nevada twisted his body, reached, and snagged the backpack. Any lingering questions Eden might have had as to Nevada's hidden injuries vanished. Except for the trapped foot, Nevada moved with supreme ease.

"What do you need?" he asked.

"Not me. You. This is trickier than I thought it would be. There's a survival blanket in the backpack. Turn the black side out."

Nevada didn't argue. Though neither of them had mentioned it, both knew it would take time to free his ankle—if it could be done at all. Even with the help of hot coffee, his big body couldn't hold heat indefinitely. Lying on the cold ground was slowly sapping his living warmth.

He opened the backpack and sorted through its contents with growing approval. Eden's fingers might be as hot and gentle as sunlight, and her breath might be as sweetly heady as wine, but she was no foolish little flower when it came to living in the wild. She had everything she might reasonably expect to need in an emergency, except a weapon.

Speculatively Nevada looked over at Baby, who was watching him with yellow eyes that missed nothing.

Maybe she doesn't need a gun after all. I'll bet Baby would go to war for her. Hell, so did I a few days ago.

I wonder if Jones has figured out yet just how lucky he was.

A snap of Nevada's wrist unrolled the survival blanket. He sat upright. The bright red of Eden's snow jacket slid away from his body as he put the empty canteen in the backpack. Wind blew across his chest, penetrating even his own shearling jacket's thick protection, making him shiver in a reflexive effort to warm himself.

Instantly Eden was at Nevada's side. She put the backpack aside and helped him to wrap the thin, incredibly warm material of the survival blanket around his body. She tried not to notice the intimacy of Nevada's breath on her face when she leaned over him, urging him to lie back. She tried not to breathe in fast and hard, taking his breath into her body, shivering at the realization that even in such a small way he was a part of her now.

"Lie down," Eden said, her voice low. "There's less of you for the wind to work on that way." Methodically she folded up her jacket and made a pillow for Nevada's head. "Here. I don't need this while I'm digging."

Nevada's senses were far too acute for him to have missed the telltale catching of Eden's breath, the new huskiness of her voice, the concern that went beyond that of one human being for another who needed help. She was intensely aware of him as a man.

Grimly Nevada tried to still his body's violent response to the knowledge that Eden was as drawn to him as he was to her. He succeeded in quelling the rush of his blood, but only up to a point. When Eden went to pull the survival blanket more snugly around his hips, she was confronted by the one thing Nevada couldn't control—the hard evidence of his response to her. The mixture of emotions on her face when she saw the fit of his jeans would have made anyone but Nevada smile.

"Reassured about my health?" he asked in a dry tone.

"Try astonished," Eden said faintly.

"Why? I'm a man, in case you hadn't noticed."

"In case *you* hadn't noticed, you're a man who is in a hell of a jam at the moment."

"So?"

"So I wouldn't think you'd be feeling very, er, lively," Eden muttered. She ducked her head, knowing her cheeks were red from much more than a cold wind.

"I accepted a long time ago that nobody gets out of life alive," Nevada said matter-of-factly. "Once you accept that you stop worrying about the details of when and where and how. Dead now or dead fifty years from now, dead is dead. And alive is alive, all the way, full max. I'm alive and you turn me on deep and quick and hard. I don't like that one damn bit, but there's nothing I can do about it."

Eden looked at him, a question in her eyes that she wouldn't ask. Nevada knew what that question was. He knew what the answer was, too.

"I don't like being turned on by you because you still believe in fairy tales like love. I know better.

That's why I told you to stay away from me. But it didn't work out that way, did it?''

Slowly Eden searched Nevada's silver-green eyes, wondering what had made him the way he was and what might heal him so that he could live completely again.

"No, it didn't work out that way," Eden said, her voice both gentle and determined. "Life is always unexpected, Nevada. That's why laughter is vital and very real. And life always seeks life. That's why love is vital and very real. Not fairy tale. Reality.''

"Sex is real," he said flatly. "Love is a game. I'm too old to play games and you're too young to do anything else, so finish digging me out of this hole and say goodbye.''

Eden looked at Nevada's icy eyes and knew that arguing with him would be futile. Yet she couldn't help reaching out to him, wanting to stroke the smooth skin of his cheek and the sleek pelt of his beard, to soothe and reassure him that he wasn't alone within the bleak world of his choosing.

With shocking speed Nevada's hand locked around Eden's wrist, preventing her from touching him.

"I'm trapped, but I'm a long way from helpless," he said coldly. "Dig or get the hell out of here and leave me alone.''

Eden had no doubt that Nevada meant it: he would sooner lie trapped in a snowstorm than submit to a kind of touching that had nothing to do with sex.

The pain that came with Eden's understanding froze the breath in her throat, making her ache for whatever wounding had caused so deep a scar to form within Nevada, sealing off all emotion except an icy kind of rage.

Sudden tears burned behind Eden's eyes. She looked away quickly, knowing Nevada would have even less use for her tears than he had for her comforting touch. Saying nothing, she came to her feet and walked away from him. The falling snow was much thicker now, limiting visibility to less than ten feet. Baby whined softly in confusion, then trotted after Eden, leaving Nevada alone beneath the lowering sky.

When Eden returned five minutes later dragging a sturdy branch taller than she was, Nevada was just raising the rifle to his shoulder.

"Save the three bullets," Eden said. "There's no one else around to care. You're stuck with me."

Nevada lowered his rifle, grabbed the jacket he had been using as a pillow and fired it in Eden's direction. "Put this on. It's cold."

Eden didn't bother to argue that she didn't need the jacket as long as she kept moving. Nor did she try to put the jacket back beneath Nevada's head as she wanted to do. She simply stepped over the bright mound of cloth and knelt near Nevada's trapped foot, examining it closely.

Nothing had changed. Just above the ankle bone, Nevada's boot was caught between heavy stones. After a struggle that left her breathing rapidly, she managed to wedge one end of the thick branch beneath the smaller of the two boulders.

Smaller, Eden thought with a fear that she concealed from Nevada. *Lord. That stone has to weigh more than Nevada and me put together. I hope the branch I found is strong enough. I hope I'm strong enough. By the time I could go for help and get back, it would be too late.*

"Do you still have feeling in your foot?" she asked tightly.

"Some."

"Too bad. This is going to hurt. Do try not to cry, cowboy. It would hurt my feelings."

Despite Nevada's determination to keep Eden at a distance, her deadpan instructions made the corner of his mouth move slightly. He shook his head and said, "I'll do my best."

"That's all I can ask, isn't it?" she said beneath her breath, thinking he couldn't hear. "Of you, of me, of anything."

Nevada did hear, but there was nothing he could say or do. Eden was right and he knew it. He just didn't like it.

Eden bent her legs, braced her shoulder beneath the branch and then began to straighten, pouring every bit of her feminine strength and determination into moving the stone, straining against a weight she was never meant to lift.

Putting his free foot against the smaller boulder, Nevada shoved hard. It had done no good before. It did no good now. He had no leverage, nothing but brute strength and no way to apply it effectively. He could wrench his trapped leg but he couldn't free himself.

Helplessly, his much greater strength useless, Nevada watched Eden strain against the stone again and again, spending herself recklessly in an attempt to free him. He cursed steadily, silently, wishing that he could do something, anything, to lighten her burden. She was too slender, too fragile, too gentle—like life itself, a flame burning against a vast icy darkness; she would break her heart and have nothing to show for it but the memory of pain and failure.

"Eden," Nevada said roughly, unable to bear watching her an instant longer. "Eden, stop!"

If she heard, she ignored him. A ragged sound was dragged from her throat as she strained to straighten her body, and in doing so force the boulder aside just a little, her muscles straining, just a few fractions of an inch—her body screaming—just enough for Nevada's foot to slide free of the rocky vise—her vision blurring and her breath burning in her chest until she sobbed.

The boulder grated as it shifted minutely.

It was all Nevada had been waiting for and more than he had thought possible. He shoved hard with his free leg against the boulder and at the same time yanked his trapped leg backward, ignoring the pain that shot through his ankle. After a few agonizing seconds his foot wrenched free of the boot and the rocky vise.

"I'm out!"

Instantly Eden let go of the branch and sank to her knees, breathing in great gulps, trying to get enough oxygen to keep the world from receding down an endless black tunnel. When she finally succeeded, she realized that Nevada was kneeling next to her, his arms around her, supporting her. With a broken sigh she leaned against his strength.

"Sorry about the boot," Eden said when she had enough breath to spare for words.

"Never fit right anyway. Too big. Damn good thing, too."

Nevada leaned to the side, snagged Eden's jacket with one hand and began stuffing her into it. When he was finished, he caught her face between his big hands.

"Do you hurt anywhere?" he asked.

She shook her head.

"Don't ever do anything that stupid again. You can tear yourself up inside and never know until it's too late," Nevada said savagely. Then, before she could say anything, he asked, "Can you walk to the cabin?"

Eden nodded.

"Get going," he said. "You're sweaty. Don't stop to rest until you're in dry clothes."

"But—"

"*Move.*"

"What about you?" Eden persisted.

"I can take care of myself."

As he spoke, Nevada automatically wiped snow off the rifle, checked the load and the firing mechanism. Satisfied that everything was in working order, he used the butt of the rifle to lever himself to his feet. Circulation was returning to his left foot, but slowly. With the renewed flowing of blood came excruciating pain. Nevada ignored it. Using the rifle as a makeshift crutch, he took a step forward.

And fell full-length in the snow.

Even as Nevada rolled onto his side to lever himself upright again, Eden spoke quickly to Baby. The wolf hit Nevada squarely in the chest, knocked him back into the snow and put one very large paw on his chest. Nevada realized instantly that he wasn't going to get up again without fighting Baby. The prospect wasn't inviting.

Eden bent over Nevada, survival blanket in hand. "Wrap up. I'll be back with the horses as soon as possible."

Before she could straighten again, Nevada's hand flashed out and snared her wrist in an immovable grip. His eyes were as cold and bleak as his voice.

"Baby or no Baby, you damn well better be in dry clothes when I see you again, lady."

4

When Eden returned leading the Appaloosa and the packhorse, she found Baby sitting next to Nevada. The animal's black paw was on the man's forearm. Yellow wolf's eyes stared into equally untamed silver-green ones. Neither one looked up when she walked in.

Eden had the distinct feeling that both males were enjoying measuring each other.

A single word called Baby off guard duty. He removed his big paw, stretched and waved his tail at Nevada in a silent offering of truce. Gravely Nevada took off his glove and held out his hand. Baby sniffed, ducked his head and offered it to be scratched.

"You're all bluff, aren't you, Baby?" Nevada asked.

A huge, gleaming wolf's grin was Baby's answer.

"Impressive. Who's your dentist?"

Eden smiled despite herself. She was still smiling when Nevada's head turned and his pale green glance raked over her, taking in every detail of her appearance. Suddenly she was very grateful the horses had continued to drift in the direction of her cabin. Otherwise she wouldn't have taken the time to change into dry clothes before coming back to Nevada. Then she would have had to explain to him why it had been more important to get back to him quickly than it had been to find dry clothes for herself. She doubted that he would have found her arguments convincing.

Nevada folded the survival blanket, stuffed it in his jacket pocket and levered himself into a standing position.

"How's your foot?" Eden asked finally.

"It's there."

"I can see that," she muttered, leading the Appaloosa closer. "Does it hurt? Do you have any feeling in it? Is it frostbitten?"

"Are you cold?" he asked, ignoring her questions.

"Damn it, Nevada, I'm not the one who's hurt!"

"Neither am I. Guess that means we're both fine. Take it easy, you knothead."

At first Eden thought Nevada was referring to her. Then she realized he was talking to the spotted horse, which had shied when Nevada came awkwardly to his feet. That was the end of Nevada's awkwardness, however. He grabbed the saddle horn and vaulted into the saddle with catlike ease.

"Hand me my rifle."

For a moment Eden was too stunned to say anything. Nevada was going to ride off into the storm without so much as a thank-you. She could handle the lack of gratitude. What made her furious was the knowledge that he wasn't nearly as "fine" as he said he was. His face was too pale and she was afraid the stain of red over his cheekbones owed more to fever than windburn. But apparently Nevada was angry about being guarded by Baby, or too proud to admit he needed anything more from her, or both.

Eden handed the rifle up to Nevada, shrugged into her backpack and walked off up the trail toward the cabin without a word, too furious to trust herself to speak. Her short temper shocked her. Normally she was the last one to lose control—but normally she wouldn't have spent the last hour digging a man out of a hole before he froze to death. And not just any man. A man she had taken one look at and gone to with the absolute certainty of water running downhill to the waiting sea.

A man who thought love was a fairy tale.

A spotted flank materialized from the snowstorm in front of Eden. The Appaloosa was standing across the trail, blocking her way. At an unseen signal from Nevada, the horse turned toward her and then stood motionless once more. Nevada kicked his stockinged foot out of the left stirrup and leaned toward Eden, holding out his left arm.

"Climb on."

"I've never ridden," she said tightly.

"I've never had a wolf sicced on me. Learn something new every day."

"I didn't sic—"

"The hell you didn't. Grab hold of me."

Eden was never sure what happened next. All she knew was that the world swung suddenly, crazily. When things settled into place again she was behind the saddle, hanging on to Nevada with both hands, for he had become the stable center of an otherwise highly mobile world.

"Well you've got the first part right," Nevada said dryly.

"What?"

"You're hanging on."

She started to speak, only to make a high, startled sound when the horse moved. Target snorted and sidestepped lightly.

"Go easy on the screaming," Nevada said. "Target is skittish. That's how we got into trouble in the first place."

"You screamed?" she retorted.

Nevada turned around enough to look at Eden. His narrowed eyes gleamed like gems between his thick black eyelashes, but she would have sworn his look was one of amusement rather than anger. She decided that she liked that particular gleam in his eyes much better than the icy distance that was his normal response to the world.

Then Nevada's glance shifted to her mouth and Eden remembered the instant when his fingertip had caressed her lips. Her heart hesitated before it beat with increased speed.

"Does that quick little tongue of yours ever get you in trouble?" he asked finally.

The intriguing rasp was back in Nevada's voice, making Eden shiver.

"Only with you," she admitted. "Normally I'm rather quiet. But I love the sound of your voice, especially when it gets all slow and deep. Like now."

His eyes narrowed even more, all amusement gone, replaced by something as elemental as a wolf's howl. The searching intensity of Nevada's glance made Eden shiver. He turned away abruptly.

"Can Baby lead us to the cabin?" Nevada asked harshly.

"Yes."

"Then tell him to do it."

"Lead us home, Baby. *Home.*"

Baby turned and began trotting along the base of the scree slope. Nevada turned Target to follow the wolf's tracks. The instant the horse began moving,

Eden made a stifled sound and clung very tightly to Nevada. He looked down, saw her arms wrapped around him, saw hands that were slender even inside gloves, knew that the hard rise of his flesh was only inches from those feminine hands, and tried not to swear aloud at the ungovernable rushing of his blood.

For several minutes there was a silence that was at least as uncomfortable as Nevada was.

"Nevada?"

He grunted.

"I wasn't making fun of your voice."

"I know."

"Then why are you angry?"

Nevada hesitated, then shrugged. "Some kinds of honesty are dangerous, Eden."

"I don't understand."

"Drop your hand down a few inches and you'll understand just fine."

Nevada's voice was remote, clipped. When Eden realized what he meant, she was glad he couldn't see her blazing cheeks. Beneath her embarrassment she was shocked. When Nevada had told her he lived every instant as though it were his last, he had meant it, and the proof was right at hand.

"Makes a girl wonder what it would take to cool you off," Eden muttered against his back, certain he wouldn't be able to hear.

He did, of course.

"Hell of a question," Nevada retorted. "Sure you want to hear the answer?"

Eden opened her mouth for an incautious reply, only to think better of it at the last instant. Before she closed her mouth, she felt the unanticipated, fragile chill of snowflakes dissolving on her tongue. Her eyes closed and she held her breath, waiting for the exquisite sensation to be repeated. As she waited, the world swayed gently beneath her and her arms clung to the living column of strength that was Nevada.

Suddenly Eden had a dizzying sense of the wonder of being alive and riding through a white storm holding on to a man whose last name she didn't even know, while snowflakes melted on her lips like secret kisses. She laughed softly and tipped her face back to the sky, giving herself to the miracle of being alive.

The sound of Eden laughing made Nevada turn toward her involuntarily, drawn by the life burning so vividly in her. He looked at her with a hunger that would have shocked her if she had seen it, but her eyes were closed beneath the tiny, biting caresses of snowflakes. When her eyes opened once more, he had already turned away.

"Nevada?"

He made a rough, questioning sound.

"What's your last name?"

"Blackthorn."

"Blackthorn," Eden murmured, savoring the name as though it were a snowflake freshly fallen onto her tongue. "What do you do when you're not rescuing maidens or falling down mountains, Nevada Blackthorn?"

"I'm *segundo* on the Rocking M when Tennessee is there. When he isn't, I'm ramrod."

"*Segundo?* Tennessee? Ramrod? Are we speaking the same language?"

The corner of Nevada's mouth lifted slightly. "A ramrod is a ranch foreman. A *segundo* is the ramrod's right-hand man. Tennessee is my brother."

"Is the Rocking M your family ranch?"

"After a fashion. We're the bastard line. The legitimate folks are the MacKenzies. Tennessee bought into the ranch when Luke MacKenzie's father was trying to drink himself to death. I own a chunk of the Devil's Peak area. Cash and Mariah gave it to me for a wedding gift."

For a few moments Eden was too stunned to breathe. "You're married?" she asked faintly.

"It was Cash and Mariah's wedding, not mine."

"They gave you a present on their wedding day," Eden said carefully.

Nevada nodded.

"Why?"

"It's a long story."

"I'm very patient."

"Could have fooled me."

"I doubt that much fools you," she said matter-of-factly.

Nevada thought of the instant he had seen Eden coming toward him in a smoky bar and his whole body had reached out to her with a primitive need that had shocked him. But he would have been a fool to talk about that, and Nevada Blackthorn was no fool.

"Mariah is Luke's sister," Nevada said. "She had a map to a gold mine that had come down through the family. The map wasn't much use because it was all blurred. I passed the map along to some people who are real good at making documents give up their secrets. When the map came back, I gave it to her. She found the mine, Cash found her, and they got married. They gave me a chunk of the mine as a wedding present."

The hint of a drawl in Nevada's voice told Eden that she was being teased. She didn't mind. She liked the thought that she could arouse that much playfulness in Nevada.

"Why do I feel you left something out?" she asked.

"Such as?"

"Such as how a *segundo* knows the kind of people who can make crummy old documents sit up and sing."

"I wasn't always a *segundo*."

Eden hesitated. The drawl was definitely gone from Nevada's voice. Even as she told herself she had no right to pry, she heard herself asking a question.

"What were you before you were a *segundo?*"

"What the Blackthorn men have been for hundreds of years—a warrior."

Vivid images from the fight in West Fork flashed before Eden's eyes, followed by other images. Nevada lying half-buried in a rock slide with a rifle in his hand. Nevada checking the rifle's firing mechanism with a few swift motions before he even tried to stand up. Nevada's bleak eyes and unsmiling mouth.

Warrior.

It explained a lot. Too much.

The vivid joy in life that Eden had experienced moments before drained away, leaving sadness in its place. Her arms tightened protectively around Nevada's powerful body as though she could somehow keep whatever might hurt him at bay. When she realized what she was doing, she didn't know whether to laugh or to weep at her own idiocy. Nevada needed protecting about as much as a bolt of lightning did.

But unlike lightning, Nevada could bleed and cry. And he had. She knew it as surely as she knew that she was alive.

Breathing Nevada's name, Eden moved her face slowly against the cool suede texture of his shearling jacket, wiping away the tears that fell when she thought of what Nevada must have endured in the years before he went to work for the Rocking M. The knowledge of his pain reached her as nothing had since the death of her little sister during Alaska's long, frigid night.

Nevada felt the surprising strength of Eden's arms holding him, heard his name breathed like a prayer into the swirling storm, sensed the aching depth of Eden's emotions. Without stopping to ask why, Nevada brought one of her gloved hands to his cheek and rubbed slowly. With a ragged sigh she relaxed against him.

For several minutes there was no sound but the tiny whispering of snowflakes over the land, the creak of cold leather, and the muffled hoofbeats of the two horses as Nevada held them to Baby's clear trail. When Nevada saw the outline of the cabin rising from the swirling veils of snow, he removed Eden's arms from around him.

"Time to let go, Eden. You're home."

Reluctantly Eden released Nevada. He swung his right leg over the front of the saddle, grabbed the saddle horn in his right hand and slid to the ground. Braced by his grip on the saddle horn, Nevada tentatively put weight on his left foot. There was pain, but he had expected it. What mattered was that the foot and ankle took his weight without giving way.

Nevada reached up, lifted Eden off the horse and lowered her to the icy ground.

"Legs still working?" he asked, holding on to her just in case.

Eden felt the hard length of Nevada pressed against her body and wondered if she would be able to breathe, much less stand. She nodded her head.

"Good. Go in and get a fire going while I take care of the horses."

"Your foot—"

"Go in and get warm," Nevada interrupted. "You'd just be in my way."

Eden would have argued, but Nevada had already turned around and begun loosening the cinch on Target's saddle. As she watched, he removed the heavy saddle easily and set it aside. There was a hesitation when he walked that reminded her of Baby—injured, but hardly disabled.

Besides, Nevada was right. She didn't know what to do with the horses.

Without a word Eden removed her backpack and jacket, shook snow from them and went into the cabin. Baby followed her in and went immediately to the coldest, draftiest spot in the cabin's single room. His thick fur had been grown for a Yukon winter. Until he shed some of his undercoat, a fire was redundant.

It took only a moment for Eden to stir the banked coals to life. That was one of the first things her parents had taught her about living in cold country—no matter how long or how short the absence was supposed to be, always leave the hearth in a state of instant readiness for the next fire. No more than a single match should be needed to bring light and warmth into a cabin.

Eden exchanged her snow boots for fleece-lined moccasins before she went to the ice chest to look for a quick meal. After sorting through the snow she had used to chill the contents of the ice chest, she found a package of chicken. Fresh vegetables were in a cardboard carton. She selected a handful, took the knife from her belt sheath and went to work.

By the time Nevada came in the front door carrying a pair of hiking boots in his hands, the cabin was warm from the fire and fragrant with the smell of chicken and dried herbs simmering together on a tall trivet over the fire. Eden looked up as Nevada took off her knit ski cap and rubbed his fingers through his short, black hair. He shrugged out of his thick shearling jacket, hung it on a nail next to hers, and walked unevenly toward the fire. Moments later he had removed his single cowboy boot and his socks and was toasting his bare feet by the flames. Bruises shadowed his left foot, which was also reddened from cold.

Eden set aside the vegetables she had been chopping and knelt next to Nevada's legs. She took his left foot between her hands and went over it with her fingertips, searching for swellings, cold spots that could be frostbite, or any other injury.

Silently Nevada's breath came in and stayed that way. Her fingers felt like gentle flames caressing his cold skin. Not by so much as a sideways look did she reveal that she knew what her touch was doing to him. The thought that Eden might be as innocent as she was alluring disturbed Nevada more deeply than her warm fingers.

"I told you I'm fine," he said. His voice was rough, irritable, for his body was reacting to Eden's touch once again.

"Your idea of fine and mine are different." Eden pressed her fingertips around a swelling. "Hurt?"

"No."

She examined his toes critically. Other than being cold, they showed no damage. She let go of his foot. Before he could prevent it, she had pressed her hand against his forehead. His temperature brought a frown to her face. She put her other hand against her own forehead for comparison.

"You're running a fever," she said.

Nevada grunted. He had been running a fever for the past hour or more. Tennessee had been right. He should have stayed out of the mountains. But he hadn't been able to. Since the fight in West Fork,

Nevada had been too restless to stick around the Rocking M's tame winter pastures.

"Are you planning on riding out into the storm as soon as your feet warm up?" Eden asked evenly, removing her hand from Nevada's forehead. "Or are you going to be sensible and wait out the storm here?"

A pale green glance fixed on Eden with searching intensity. The warning Nevada had spoken to her once before hung in the air between them: *Stay away from me, Eden. I want you more than all the men in that bar put together.*

"Aren't you nervous about being alone with me in a cabin at the end of the world?" Nevada asked softly.

"No."

"You damned well should be."

"Why?"

Nevada said something rude under his breath.

"I know you want me," Eden said simply. "I also know you won't rape me. And not because of Baby. The way you fight, you probably could take care of a pack of wolves. But if I said no, you wouldn't so much as touch me. Even if I said yes..." She shrugged.

"You have more faith in me than I do."

Eden's smile was as beautiful as it was sad. "Yes, I know."

She stood up and went back to chopping vegetables.

Broodingly Nevada looked around the cabin. Once it had been a base camp for hunters who were less interested in fine decorator touches than in solid shelter from storms. In the far corner of the room, next to Baby, there was a small potbellied stove. A section of chimney pipe was missing. Obviously Eden had decided it would be easier to stay warm near the big fieldstone hearth than to fix the stove's broken chimney.

Narrowed green eyes inventoried the contents of the room in a sweeping glance that missed nothing. Bedroll and mattress laid out, clothes either hung on nails or put neatly into the rough-hewn dresser, kitchen implements stacked on overturned cartons, camp chairs, a small can of oil set near the kitchen pump, a bucket of water to prime the pump, a kerosene lantern as well as a battery model; it was apparent that Eden was at home in the Spartan shelter.

Eden walked across the room, pushed a thick, faded curtain aside, and looked out. Snow was coming down thick and hard. Saying nothing, she let herself out of the cabin's only door and closed it behind her. Instantly Baby came to his feet and went to stand by the door. A minute later the door opened again. Eden came in, dragging Nevada's packsacks behind. She kicked the door shut.

Without the awkwardness of wearing only one cowboy boot to hamper him, Nevada moved with startling speed and only the slightest limp. He took her hands from the canvas packsacks.

"Put your bed near the hearth," Eden said. "The cabin gets cold by dawn."

"Next time let me get my own gear. These sacks are too heavy for you."

Eden gave him a look out of hazel eyes that were almost molten gold with reflected flames. "You've been hurt and you're running a fever," she said with careful patience. "That makes us about even in the strength department."

"Bull," Nevada said succinctly.

With no visible effort he lifted both sacks, walked across the room and dumped the sacks to one side of the hearth. Eden stared. She knew how heavy those bags were. She'd had a hard time simply dragging them into the cabin.

"Okay, I was wrong," she said, throwing up her hands. "You can jump tall buildings in a single bound and catch bullets in your bare hands."

"Bare teeth," Nevada said without looking up.

"What?"

"You catch bullets with your teeth."

"You may," she retorted, "but I'm not that stupid."

"The hell you aren't." Nevada lifted his head and pinned her with a cougar's pale green glance. "You're alone in the middle of a snowstorm with a man who gets hard every time you lick your lips. And you *trust* me. That, lady, is damned stupid."

5

Sensing that something was wrong, Eden awoke with a start. In the silent spaces between gusts of wind, she heard a man speaking in broken phrases, fragmented names, snatches of language that had no rational meaning. But they made sense emotionally. Someone was hurt, trapped, dying....

And it was happening over and over again.

Nevada.

Quickly Eden sat up and looked across the hearth to the place where Nevada had set up his bedroll and mattress. The room was so dark that she could see only an outline, a darker black that indicated Nevada was still there. The cold in the room was the penetrating chill of a winter that would not release the land into spring's life-giving embrace.

Without leaving her sleeping bag, Eden stirred the fire into life and added fuel. Flames surged up, bringing light and heat into the room. A swift glance told Eden that Nevada was only half-covered, restless, caught in the grip of fever or nightmare or both.

Eden unzipped her sleeping bag and slid out. Her double-layer, silk-and-wool ski underwear turned aside the worst of the chill, but the floor was icy on her bare feet. Silently she knelt next to Nevada, watching the contours of his face emerge from the darkness as flames licked over the wood.

A combination of stark shadows, black beard, shifting orange flames and physical tension drew Nevada's features into lines as harsh as they were compelling to Eden's senses. His torso was lean, muscular, highlighted by fire and midnight swirls of hair. He wore no shirt, nothing to keep the cold at bay.

Eden knelt at Nevada's side. As she had earlier in the day, she put her hand on his forehead to gauge his temperature.

The world exploded.

Within the space of two seconds Eden was jerked over Nevada's body, thrown on her back and stretched helplessly beneath his far greater weight while a hot steel band closed around her throat. In the wavering light Nevada's eyes were those of a trapped cougar, luminous with fire, bottomless with shadow, inhuman.

"*Nevada . . .*" Eden whispered, all she could say, for the room was spinning away.

Instantly the pressure vanished. Eden felt the harsh shudder that went through Nevada's body before he rolled aside, releasing her from his weight. She shivered with the cold of the cabin floor biting into her flesh, and with another, deeper cold, the winter chill that lay at the center of Nevada's soul.

"Next time you want to wake me up, just call my name. Whatever you do, don't touch me. Ever."

Nevada's voice was as remote as his eyes had been.

"That's the problem, isn't it?" Eden asked after a moment, her voice husky.

"What?"

"Touching. You haven't had enough of it. Not the caring kind, the warm kind, the gentle kind."

"Warmth is rare and temporary. Cruelty and pain aren't. A survivor hones his reflexes accordingly. I'm a survivor, Eden. Don't ever forget it. If you catch me off guard I could hurt you badly and never even mean to."

Eden closed her eyes and shivered against the icy cold. Suddenly she felt herself lifted again. She made a startled sound and stiffened.

"It's all right," Nevada said calmly. "I'm wideawake now. Turn your face toward the fire."

The difference in temperature between the floor and Nevada's bed was disorienting. Eden let out a broken sigh of relief at the warmth and turned her face toward the dancing flames. When she felt Nevada's hand at her throat once more, she gave him a startled look. Nevada didn't notice. He was carefully peeling down the mock-turtleneck collar of her top. Gently his hand slid up beneath her chin, urging her to turn more fully toward the fire.

As Eden turned, a necklace of fine gold chain spilled from the scarlet fabric into Nevada's hand, drawn by the fragile weight of the ring she wore as a pendant. The shimmer of metal caught his eye. He looked more closely and saw that the ring was made of fine strands of smoothly braided gold. When he realized that the ring was too small to be worn by anyone but a very young child, he tipped his palm and let the gold slide away.

Firelight revealed no marks on the creamy surface of Eden's throat. With devastating gentleness Nevada's fingertips traced the taut tendons and satin skin. The startled intake of her breath followed by the visible, rapid surge of her pulse made Nevada's body tighten in a wild, sweeping rush that was becoming familiar to him around Eden.

Even as Nevada told himself he should be grateful that Eden's response to him came from fear rather than desire, he knew he wasn't grateful. He wanted nothing so much as to soothe with his tongue the tender flesh he had savaged, and then go on to find even warmer, more tender flesh and know its sweetness, as well.

But even if he were fool enough to start something he wasn't going to finish, Eden wouldn't be fool enough to want him. She finally understood what he was: a warrior, not a knight in shining armor.

Eden trembled again.

"Don't worry. I won't hurt you now," Nevada said.

The subdued rasp in his voice was like a hidden caress, making Eden ache to know more of his touch.

"I know," she whispered.

"Do you? You're trembling."

"I'm not used to... this."

"Take my word for it," Nevada said sardonically, "nearly being strangled isn't the sort of thing you get used to." His fingertips probed lightly at her soft skin. "Tender?"

Eden shook her head.

"Does it hurt when you talk?" he asked.

"No."

"Are you sure?"

She nodded.

"I don't believe you."

"But it's true," Eden said. "You didn't hurt me."

The throaty intimacy of her voice made Nevada burn. Very carefully he lifted his hand from Eden's warmth. He sat up in a tangle of sleeping bag and blankets, bringing her upright with him. The easy way he handled her weight served to underline his strength and her vulnerability—a vulnerability she stubbornly refused to acknowledge.

As Nevada released Eden, she reached up and put her palm on his forehead. He jerked back.

"You were lucky, Eden. Very lucky. Don't push it."

"You should take your own advice."

Nevada gave her a narrow look. "Meaning?"

"You're running a fever, but you plan on getting up at dawn and riding out of here."

Nevada shrugged. "I'll see what it looks like in the morning."

"White," Eden said succinctly.

"What?"

"It will look white. All of it. Even if it stops snowing, you won't be able to tell. The wind will strip off the new snow and blow it everywhere. White on white, sky and ground, everything and everywhere. If you don't believe me, listen to the wind. You would be a fool to go anywhere tomorrow, and survivors aren't fools."

Nevada turned and looked at Eden with unfathomable eyes. "Get back in your own bed. Fever or no fever, there's nothing you can do for me."

After a long, tight moment, Eden went back to her sleeping bag, crawled in and shivered until she was warm once more.

"Nevada?"

He grunted unencouragingly.

"What were you dreaming about?"

"Was I dreaming?"

"Yes. That's what woke me up."

Silence.

"Do you dream like that often?" she persisted.

"I don't know."

"How can you not know?"

"Survivors don't remember their dreams. That's how we stay sane."

Nevada rolled over and was asleep within moments.

Eden lay awake for a long time, thinking about survivors and listening to the wind rearrange layers of snow over the frozen land.

"Baby, give them to me," Eden coaxed.

Baby moved just beyond her reaching fingers. Yellow eyes gleamed with unmistakable mischief. From either side of Baby's long muzzle dangled Nevada's socks. Plainly the wolf had no intention of giving up his prize.

Eden made a sudden grab. Baby danced backward and then half crouched, his muzzle on his front paws, his hindquarters in the air, his tail waving with delight at having suckered his mistress into playing with him.

Nevada looked up from stacking firewood next to the hearth, where the heat could dry out wood newly brought in from the snow.

"Good thing I have extra socks," he said. "Look's like that pair is a goner."

"Baby knows better, at least with my socks," Eden said, exasperated. "Guess he figured yours were fair game. Baby, *drop.*"

Yellow eyes met hazel ones for a long moment. With a startlingly human look of disappointment, Baby opened his mouth. Socks dropped to the floor, no worse for the time spent in a wolf's jaws. Eden picked up the socks, tossed them in Nevada's direction, and rubbed both hands through Baby's thick neck fur, praising him for giving up his prize. Baby burrowed into her touch in return, stropping himself against her like a huge cat, plainly enjoying the physical contact.

Nevada watched through hooded eyes, oddly moved by the sight of the big, frankly savage-looking beast being petted by a woman who weighed less than the animal did and was considerably less well equipped to defend herself. As she buried her face in the wolf's fur, it didn't seem to occur to Eden that those long jaws and steel muscles could tear her apart.

You're a fool, Eden Summers. A sweet fool, but a fool just the same. You trust too much.

Baby made a sound that was a cross between a chesty growl and a throaty yap as he half crouched again, waving his tail, vibrating with a desire for energetic play after being penned up by the storm. Eden laughed and shoved against the wolf with both hands, sending him skidding across the smooth wooden floor. With a powerful scrambling of legs, Baby stopped his backward motion and romped toward Eden, who was braced on hands and knees, waiting for Baby's charge. Instead of running into Eden head-on, the wolf turned at the last instant, buffeting her with his shoulder.

If Eden hadn't been prepared, she would have been bowled over, but this was an old game for the two of them. She gave as good as she got, throwing her weight behind her shoulder as Baby raced by, sending him scrambling for purchase on the slick wood floor. Eden barely had a chance to recover her own balance before Baby was back for more. She survived a few more glancing passes before the wolf's greater strength and coordination sent her rolling.

Instantly Baby pivoted, scrambled for traction and started after his laughing mistress. Eden had just enough time to brace herself again before more than a hundred and thirty pounds of muscle and fur bounded into her. She shoved hard against Baby, knowing she was going to go spinning again but determined to give the wolf a good tussle.

Before Baby's shoulder could connect with Eden, she was lifted and set down behind Nevada. The wolf hit the man instead. Two strong hands shoved hard against steel muscles and thick fur. Baby went spinning and sliding across the cabin floor. He recovered, gave Nevada a look of glittering delight, and came full tilt across the cabin floor toward the man.

This time Nevada waited on all fours as Eden had. Muscular shoulder met muscular shoulder, Baby rebounded and went sliding and scrambling across the floor. When the wolf regained his balance, he gave Nevada a laughing, long-tongued grin and charged once more, holding back nothing of his strength as he had earlier in the game with Eden.

"You're in for it now, Nevada," Eden crowed breathlessly. "Baby hasn't had a decent wrestling match since Mark broke his arm, so Baby's loaded for bear—and with that sleek beard, you're looking like bear to him."

Just as Nevada turned to ask who Mark was, Baby sprang. Nevada went down in a tangle of arms, furry legs and waving black tail. Laughing hard at Nevada's comeuppance, trying to catch her breath at the same time, Eden sank onto her bed and applauded while wolf and warrior romped.

And a romp it was. Nevada and Baby caromed off ice chest and walls, supply sacks and packsaddle, firewood and empty water bucket. The room became a shambles of its former neat condition. Yet no matter how fast or exciting the wrestling became, both wolf and warrior kept individual weapons carefully sheathed. Fangs never sank into flesh, nor did steel fingers gouge. Claws might rake the floor, but nothing else. Unarmed combat tactics remained unused.

Finally Nevada wrestled Baby to the floor and pinned him there, both of them breathing hard. The wolf relaxed, baring his throat and belly to the warrior, accepting the end of the game. Nevada shook Baby gently by the scruff, spoke to him calmly, and released him. Baby sprang up, shook himself thoroughly, and stood panting and grinning up at Nevada. The left side of Nevada's mouth kicked up slightly in return. He sat on his heels and took the wolf's big head in his hands, rubbing the base of the erect ears and smoothing the thick fur.

"You're one hell of a fighter, old man," Nevada said quietly.

Baby's head turned. Big jaws gently closed over Nevada's right hand, then released him.

"That's meant to reassure you," Eden explained in a soft voice. "It's a wolf's kiss. Wolves aren't quite the same as dogs. They require different things from their friends, whether four-footed or two."

"What should I do to reassure Baby in return?"

"You already have."

"How?"

"You accepted his surrender, let him go with his dignity intact, and then praised him with your touch and your voice." Eden paused thoughtfully. "You read Baby very well, Nevada. Have you ever worked with undomesticated animals?"

"All my life."

"Really? What kind?"

"Men."

Eden started to laugh before she realized that there was more truth than humor in what Nevada said. Then she laughed anyway, a bittersweet and very human laughter, accepting what could not be changed in the nature of man and beast.

"Maybe if men had their signals of dominance and submission as well worked out as wolves," Eden said, "there would be fewer wars."

"I suspect we had our signals straight once. Then we got civilized and it all went to hell."

Nevada stood and stretched. His glance fell on the upside-down water bucket, the packsaddle standing on end, and other signs of the romp. The corners of his eyes crinkled slightly.

"Looks like I have my work cut out for me before we go cat hunting," Nevada said.

Eden's breath caught. She smiled brilliantly and said in a husky voice, "Thank you."

He gave her a sideways glance. "For not leaving you to clean up the mess?"

"No," she said, dismissing the room with a wave of her hand. "For staying here one more day. I know you think I'm silly for worrying about you, but I'm not. Spring, especially in a cold country, is the hardest season on animals. No matter how strong you are, the huge temperature swings stress your body. I've seen flu turn into pneumonia . . ."

Eden's voice dipped, almost broke and then steadied. "Anyway, if you had ridden off today I would have worried. Now I'll know where you are and if your fever is really gone."

"And if I've managed to stay on top of Target this time?" Nevada said dryly.

Eden's laugh was as soft as the creamy skin of her throat. She started to speak but could think of nothing to say except the truth.

"I'm glad you're staying, Nevada. Not just for my peace of mind, either. Even with fresh snow, no wind, and Baby's nose, finding cougars out there won't be easy. I suspect you're a good tracker."

"I get by."

The buried drawl in Nevada's voice told Eden that he was amused by something. She smiled slightly. "I'll just bet you do. You don't miss much, do you?"

"No."

Eden didn't need to be told any more. Nevada had lived on the razor edge of awareness for so long that he had forgotten there was any other way to live.

"I'll put your skills to work every chance I get," Eden said. "There's so little time."

"I heard you'd be here until June. At least, I heard the government cat expert would be here. That's you, isn't it?"

"After a fashion, but probably there will be more than one cat expert coming and going. My grant money is private, administered through the university at Boulder, but I'm working in conjunction with a federal study of cougars. The whole study will cover a decade. My part will last only as long as the tracking snows do, unless I find a female that's denned up with cubs. Then I might be able to stretch things into May or June."

Nevada bent over, righted the packsaddle with an easy motion and asked, "What is your part?"

"A feasibility study."

"Of what?"

"Whether it's possible to monitor cougars without drugging them, putting on bulky radio collars, and then turning the cats loose to lead a supposedly normal life."

"Yeah, I always wondered how many animals the scientists lost that way," Nevada said dryly. "Drugs are tricky things, especially with cats. As for the radio collars..."

He shrugged, bent over a bedroll and began putting it back together with the smooth, efficient motions of a man who has done a task so often he no longer has to think about it. Eden worked alongside Nevada, watching him from the corners of her eyes, fascinated by his unconscious grace and his casual acceptance of his own physical strength.

"What about the radio collars?" Eden asked, realizing belatedly that Nevada had stopped talking and was watching her watch him.

"I'm no specialist," Nevada said, looking away from Eden, straightening a blanket with a casual snap of his wrist, "but I've noticed one thing about wild animals. If there's anything different about an animal, the others shun him. Or they attack him. Makes me wonder if anyone has thought about that when they wrap a few pounds of brightly packaged radio collar around a wild animal and turn it loose. Then the specialists come back every few days or weeks in a helicopter or a small plane and buzz the hell out of the local wildlife trying to track down the radio collar's signal."

"Somebody around here must have thought about it," Eden said. She knelt and began stacking firewood that had been scattered when Nevada had rolled into it. "Dr. Martin said my particular part of the grant money came from one of the local ranchers." Suddenly she turned and looked at Nevada. "Was it you?"

He hesitated fractionally in the act of righting the water bucket, then shrugged and said, "I'm a cowhand, not a rancher. Luke and Ten own the land."

Eden waited, certain that she was right. Only someone who respected and understood wildlife would have given money for a study that didn't disrupt the animals' normal lives. It was obvious that Nevada felt an unusual affinity for wild animals. She had never seen Baby take to a person with such ease.

"Both Luke and Ten admire the cougars, but they have their hands full raising kids and cattle," Nevada continued, "and at the same time they're protecting and excavating some of the Anasazi sites at September Canyon. On a ranch there's never enough money to do everything that should be done."

"So you paid for part of the grant."

Again, Nevada shrugged. "The cougars are staging a comeback around here. Now, I believe the cats live on wild food rather than on Rocking M beef, but I couldn't prove it even though I spent a lot of time chasing cats when I should have been chasing cattle. So I took some of the money from the gold mine Mariah found and told the university to find an expert who could study our cougars without drugging or harassing them."

"I won't drug the cats," Eden said. "But having Baby on their trail might constitute harassment."

Nevada's mouth shifted subtly beneath his beard. He reached down and ruffled the wolf's sleek fur. Baby leaned into the touch, enjoying it.

"Dogs have been chasing cats at least as long as men have been chasing women," Nevada said, giving Eden a brief, sidelong look. "I think the cats might even get a kick out of a good race. Cougars will run like hell, but once they're up in a tree, they relax. Hell, I've seen more than one cougar curl up for a nap in some tall timber while a pack of hounds went crazy barking down below." Frowning thoughtfully, Nevada turned away from scratching Baby's ears. "That reminds me—does Baby ever bark?"

"Rarely."

Nevada's mouth flattened. "Then you've got the wrong hunting dog no matter how good Baby's nose is. A cougar will run from a barking dog, even if it's no bigger than a Scottish terrier. But a dog that doesn't bark will be attacked, no matter how big it is."

"Don't worry. Cats are the exception to Baby's code of silence. When he's on a hot cat trail, Baby makes more noise than a pack of foxhounds."

"Good." Nevada looked around the room, which was neat once more. "That leaves just one other thing to settle before we go hunting. Who's Mark?"

Eden looked up, surprised by the sudden edge in Nevada's voice. "What?"

"Baby's wrestling partner," Nevada said flatly. "The man who broke his arm."

"Oh. That Mark. He's my brother."

Nevada grunted. "How many Marks do you know?"

"Just two."

Nevada waited, watching Eden with pale green eyes as she stacked the last piece of firewood, stood up and dusted her hands on her pants.

"The second Mark was my fiancé for a time," she continued. "Then he discovered that being lifelong friends wasn't the same thing as really wanting a woman. He took one look at Karen and knew something important had been missing from our relationship. They were married a month later."

Nevada had had a lot of practice reading people. He saw no indications of distress in Eden as she talked about her broken engagement. Her voice was even, supple, almost amused. Not at all the way it had been when she had discussed flu turning into pneumonia.

"You sound like you didn't mind losing Mark to another girl," Nevada said, walking slowly across the room toward Eden.

"I didn't lose him. We're still friends."

Skepticism showed in the arch of Nevada's black eyebrows. Eden watched with widening eyes as he came closer and then closer still, not stopping until he was so close that she could feel the heat from his big body.

"It's true," she said, puzzled by Nevada's intensity. "Mark and I are still friends."

"Then you were never lovers."

Eden made a soft, startled sound deep in her throat. "How did you know?"

"Easy. Once a man had you, he'd want you again with every breath he took." Nevada shrugged, but the silver-green intensity of his eyes didn't diminish. "Which means Mark never had you, because he let you go."

6

The elemental harmonics of a wolf's howl shivered over the land before dissipating on the wind. Nevada froze, listening with every fiber of his body. The sound came again, rising and falling, a song sung to the primal memories that existed in every human soul. The eerie ululation faded into the wind. Silence reigned once more.

"A wolf's howl has to be one of the most beautiful sounds on earth," Nevada said in a hushed voice.

Eden didn't disagree. She had heard only one thing more compelling—Nevada's deep voice when he looked at her and told her that any man who had her would never let her go. Even now she could hardly believe Nevada had said it, meant it, and then turned away, picked up his rifle and calmly asked her if she was ready to go hunting.

The memories made Eden's fingers tremble as she cupped her hands around her mouth and answered Baby with a call that was more musical than a shout and less structured than a yodel. When she finished, Nevada looked at her expectantly.

"Baby's just checking in," Eden explained. "Now we know where he is and he knows where we are. No cats, though."

Nevada nodded. "He won't hit cougar sign on this side of the stream unless a new cat has moved in since I was here last. Once Baby gets to the other side of the stream, though, it shouldn't be long before he hits a trail. A young female staked out her territory there two years ago."

"How young? Did she have cubs?"

"The first year she didn't mate. But this year there was some real caterwauling around here for the two weeks she and her mate traveled together." The left corner of Nevada's mouth lifted a bit and he added blandly, "Seems like the young females always scream the loudest."

"There's a reason they scream," Eden said before she could think better of it.

"Really? What?"

All right, how am I going to get out of this one? Eden asked herself wryly, caught between embarrassment and amusement.

"Er, take my word for it," she said, knowing her cheeks were bright with something more than cold.

"Give me some words and I'll see how I take them."

"Better yet," Eden said quickly, thinking of a graceful exit from the topic, "I'll give you a textbook on cat anatomy."

"Did you bring it with you?"

She sighed. "No."

"Then we're back to words."

Eden suspected she was being teased. Nevada's eyes had a definite crinkle at the corners. She took a deep breath, reminded herself that she and Nevada were both adults, and began speaking as though she were in a graduate seminar.

"Male cats are built to begin, but not to end, copulation. Therefore, disengagement must be rather uncomfortable for the females."

Nevada gave Eden a sideways glance. "I'm missing something."

"Barbs," she said succinctly.

The sleek black of Nevada's beard shifted a bit as his mouth quirked, but he said only, "Can't be all that bad—"

"Spoken like a true male," she muttered.

"—because the older females keep coming back for more," Nevada finished, ignoring Eden's interruption.

She saw the gleam in his eyes and knew that Nevada was teasing her. She struggled not to laugh. It was impossible. The wicked light in Nevada's eyes reminded her of Baby's when he had danced up to her with a mouthful of forbidden socks and lured her into play.

Nevada listened to the rippling warmth of Eden's laughter and silently decided that it was even more beautiful than a wolf's wild song. He fought the impulse to put an arm around Eden and hug her to his side, and then to bend down and taste lips whose tempting curves haunted him at every moment.

I should have left yesterday, storm or no storm. If I stay much longer I'm going to reach out and take what I need more than I need air.

Having her would be like sinking into fire, all hot and clean and wild, no boundaries, no restraints, nothing but the two of us and the fire burning higher and higher....

A wolf's howl leaped and twisted in the wild silence, calling to them, demanding their attention.

"He's found cat sign!" Eden said. She looked eagerly around the landscape, trying to decide on the quickest route to Baby. "It could be bobcat, I suppose."

"I'm betting it isn't," Nevada said promptly, heading toward the creek. "There's a big old fir on top of that rise. The lady cougar likes to lie up beneath the lowest limbs and watch the land."

"Hurry," Eden said, following. "Once Baby starts running, we may not see him again until he's ready to come into the cabin and chew the ice out from between his toes."

Nevada moved swiftly down the slope toward the creek that gleamed blackly between low banks of snow. Despite the snow that had fallen yesterday, neither Nevada nor Eden needed the snowshoes they had tied to their backpacks. Only in the steepest ravines or in the most dense forest was snowpack more than six inches deep. Yesterday's storm had filled in minor hollows and ripples, leaving behind a pristine surface that took and held tracks as though it had been designed for just that purpose.

Baby howled again. Then came a series of short, excited barks.

"He's seen the cat!" Eden said.

"Will he call off?"

"Doubt it. Not after being shut up in a car and then in the cabin."

Nevada leaped the stream with a lithe power that made Eden think enviously of a cougar. She judged the distance to the other side and skidded to a stop. If she jumped, she'd be asking for an icy dunking on landing and a twisted ankle in the bargain.

"Go on," she urged. "I'll catch up as soon as I find a safe way across. Try to get a look at the cat so we can identify it if we see it again. Once they're forty feet up a tree, cats are darned hard to see, much less identify, even with binoculars."

Nevada hesitated for only an instant before he took off up the rise toward a big fir tree.

Eden trotted—and occasionally slid and slithered—along the side of the creek, muttering about boulders concealed by snow and other traps for the unwary. Finally she came to a place where sun or wind or both had cleaned the rocks of snow. She jumped from boulder to boulder across the stream and headed up the rise. Soon she was following Nevada's tracks.

Lord, that man runs like a big cat. No slipping, no struggling for balance, nothing but clean, long-legged strides.

Baby's barks were faint now, continuous, and very excited.

Sounds like the cat is up a tree. That was fast work. Hope Nevada got a look before it was too late.

When Eden got to the top of the rise, she saw the place where the cougar had been stretched out on the ground beneath a low limb, watching the world in relaxed silence until a loudmouthed black wolf had appeared. Then all hell had cut loose. The cougar—for the size of the tracks left no doubt that a cougar had made them rather than a bobcat—had exploded out of cover, sending a shower of snow from lower branches. The cat had hit its full running stride instantly, racing over the sparsely wooded slope, heading uphill as cats always did when pursued.

Baby's barking ended abruptly, telling Eden that Nevada had already caught up. Cocking her head, Eden listened, heard nothing to indicate that the chase was anything but over, and returned her attention to a particularly fine set of tracks the cougar had left. Baby wasn't going anywhere now. Neither was the cat. The tracks, however, were at the mercy of the rising wind and the sun. She had to photograph the tracks before they lost their fine, crisp edges.

Automatically Eden took off her backpack, opened it and went to work. She pulled out camera and ruler, lined up the ruler close to the tracks, adjusted the camera's macrozoom lens and triggered the shutter. In the forest silence, the *snick, snick, snick* of the shutter and the faint rubbing of her clothes against the snow when she knelt were the only sounds. When she was through measuring and photographing the prints, she took out a notebook and began to record information.

Eden was halfway through a sentence when she had the distinct feeling of being watched. She spun around. Nevada was standing less than an arm's length away.

"Lord, Nevada, you're a quiet man!"

"Sorry. I didn't mean to startle you."

Eden pushed a deep breath out of her lungs to slow her hammering heart, took a better grip on her pencil and resumed recording her observations.

"Did you get a look at the cougar?" she asked.

"It's the young female. She wintered well. Coat is thick and smooth, no sign of hesitation in her stride. I can't be positive, but I think she's nursing cubs. Her teats were swollen."

With a startled sound Eden jammed her notebook and pencil into her jacket pocket. "I'd better go call off Baby. I don't want a new mother getting panicked."

Nevada lifted Eden's backpack and started back up the trail. "Don't worry about the cougar. Last time I saw her, she was stretching out on a limb to watch Baby jawing at her from below."

"Will I be able to see her?" Eden asked, excited.

"Some."

"How much?"

"The black tip of her long, thick tail."

"Figures," Eden muttered. "Seems like all I ever see of my cats are silent ghosts sliding away at the corner of my eyes."

When Nevada and Eden arrived at the fir where Baby was leaping and yapping, not even the tip of a tail was to be seen. Eden called off Baby and went to work examining the tree through binoculars. Finally she spotted the cougar partway up the big evergreen.

The cat was indeed stretched out along a hefty limb, watching the activity below through half-closed eyes. So well did the cougar screen herself with greenery that Eden wouldn't have seen the animal at all if she hadn't yawned. The motion revealed an astonishing length of pink tongue, as well as teeth of intimidating size and sharpness. The yawn ended, the jaws began closing, and the pink tongue vanished.

An instant later, so did the cougar. Occasional tufts of snow rained down, revealing that the cat was still moving somewhere within the drooping, multiple arms of the tree. No matter how hard Eden looked through the binoculars, she couldn't see so much as a patch of the cat's thick, tawny fur.

Baby whined coaxingly, tired of having to be silent.

"Nope," Eden said to Baby as she lowered the binoculars. "Fun's over." She turned to Nevada. "Are you sure she was nursing?"

"It's more of a hunch. She's healthy, but tires fast, even for a cat. She took to a tree real quick, even though Baby wasn't close to her." Nevada shrugged and squinted up into the tree with pale green eyes. "I'm no expert, though."

"I'll take your instincts over the expertise of anyone I've ever worked with. You're a very noticing kind of man." Eden reached for her pack, which Nevada was still holding in one big hand. "Let's try backtracking from that big fir. If you're right about her having cubs, she'll have a den, too. Maybe we can find it."

"It would make our work a lot easier," Nevada agreed.

Eden heard the word *our* and felt a shiver of pleasure travel through her body. But if Nevada realized what he had implied, nothing was revealed on his face.

"The cougars over on the other side of MacKenzie Ridge," he continued, "have much bigger territories. Up here, the countryside supports more deer, so the cats get by with a lot less land. Even so, they can cover twenty, thirty miles a day looking for prey or for a mate or just keeping their boundary markers fresh."

"Speaking of food, my lunch is in my backpack." Eden tugged discreetly at one of the straps Nevada held.

"Hungry?"

Eden looked up. Nevada's light green eyes were very clear, the lashes surrounding them were ragged slices of midnight, and he was watching her with an intensity that made her breath shorten.

"Yes, I'm . . . hungry."

Her voice was too husky, but Eden was helpless to change it. Something in Nevada's eyes was making her blood shimmer wildly through her body, leaving chaos in its wake. She would have moved, but felt unable to so much as take a step. Motionless she waited for him to say something.

"Nevada?" she whispered finally, looking up at him, wondering what was wrong, why she felt as though she were on the edge of a cliff and had only to spread her wings and fly...or fall endlessly, spinning away into infinity like a snowflake on the wind.

Nevada saw the yearning and uncertainty in Eden's wide hazel eyes, hissed a searing word between his teeth and let go of her backpack. The straps slid through her fingers. She grabbed awkwardly with both hands, but it was Nevada's extraordinary quickness that kept the pack from being dumped into the snow. Instead of giving the backpack to Eden, he slung it over one shoulder and turned back the way they had come.

For a moment Eden was too unsettled to follow. She watched Nevada stride through the widely spaced trees. He moved with a strength and silence that should have frightened her, but did not. His male grace and power tugged at her senses, just as the realization that she had never seen Nevada in any but dark clothes tugged at her emotions.

He wants me. He's never made any secret of it. So why won't he even kiss me?

The thought of being kissed by Nevada made Eden's blood shimmer wildly once more. Her breath came in hard, ragged, and she wanted nothing so much at that instant as the feel of Nevada's lips on her own.

Lord, if Mark had had this effect on me, we'd be married by now, with kids in the bargain.

The thought of having Nevada's children went through Eden like lightning, shaking her—another human being with a smile like hers and black hair like his, another person with curiosity and discipline and maybe, just maybe, a boy with his father's smooth coordination, his strength, his restraint.

Eden's breath rushed out, leaving her almost dizzy. She blinked and took several slow breaths as she looked around in the manner of a person who has awakened in a strange land. The snow-brushed trees were unchanged, the white glitter of sunswept snow was the same, and the tracks still showed as blue-white marks in the snow. Nothing in the world around her had changed.

Yet everything had changed. For the first time in Eden's life, her own inner world, the untouched, unviolated privacy of her dreams, had been transformed by the presence of a man.

I'm falling in love with Nevada.

No. Scratch that. It's past tense, over and done with, and I was the last one to know.

Baby whined and nudged Eden's hand. Absently she stroked his big head. He ducked, caught her gloved hand in his mouth and tugged. Immediately he had her full attention.

"You're right, Baby. It's time we left the mama cougar in peace. Or is it lunch you're after, hmm? Does your sharp nose know that all the food left with Nevada? Or do you sense that he's making off with my heart as well as my backpack?"

Yellow eyes watched Eden alertly.

"Yes, I know," she said in a low voice. "It's stupid of me to let someone walk off with something that vital. But my lack of sense is nothing new. A smart girl would have followed everyone's advice and let you die after finding you in that trap, rather than take a chance on getting savaged while trying to teach a wild young mostly-wolf to trust people again."

Baby cocked his head to the side, listening to Eden with every fiber of his mostly-wolf being. Then he made a soft sound deep in his throat and turned his head to look out across the land.

"Okay, boy, I get the message," Eden said. She swept her arm in the direction in which Nevada had gone. "Go catch up with lunch."

It was like releasing a catapult. Within three seconds Baby had reached his full stride and was running with his belly low to the ground and his tail streaming out like a dark banner. Eden followed more slowly, needing time to get a better grip on her unsettled and unsettling thoughts.

Nevada won't be an easy man to love. He's a winter man, shut down deep inside, waiting for a spring that hasn't come.

On the heels of Eden's thought came another, a realization as unflinching as winter itself.

Don't kid yourself. You're going into this with your eyes wide open or you're not going at all. Nevada isn't waiting for spring. He probably doesn't even believe spring exists. That's quite a difference.

It's a difference that could break my heart.

Yet even knowing that, Eden could no more walk away from Nevada now than she had been able to walk away years ago from a wild young wolf made savage by pain.

7

With unnerving quickness Nevada pushed back from the long table where everyone on the Rocking M ate dinner.

"Good God, Nevada," Ten muttered as his brother turned away to leave. "You're as jumpy as a long-tailed cat in a roomful of rocking chairs. If you're so worried about that female that you can't sit through a whole meal, go check on her."

The ranch hands sitting around the Rocking M's table became silent. Nevada had indeed been edgy for the five days since he had ridden back down out of Wildfire Canyon missing one boot. Privately the hands had speculated that Target had dumped his rider down the scree slope out of self-preservation, but not one of the men had offered that theory within Nevada's hearing. After learning about the modern-day fight at the OK Corral, the cowhands had been very careful to give Nevada all the room he might need, and then extra space for good measure.

Nevada turned around with feline quickness. Narrowed, ice-green eyes focused on Ten.

"What female?" Nevada asked softly.

"The mama cougar, who else?" Ten said blandly as he poured gravy over his second serving of chicken. "We all know how worried you get over mothers." He winked at Mariah, who was at the moment very rounded out by her twins. "You always know women are pregnant before they do, and then you nag them like a maiden aunt to get them to take proper care of themselves. It's a wonder the human race ever got gestated without your help."

Nevada grunted.

Ten's wife, Diana, smiled at her plate. Carla, Mariah and Diana were all touched by Nevada's concern for them and their babies. It was so unexpected coming from a man as hard as Nevada was.

"Go ahead and check on that female again," Ten continued, carefully not looking at his brother, for Nevada wouldn't have missed the amused warmth in Ten's gray eyes. "We've got eleven hands now and two more coming tomorrow. Won't even miss you. Right, Luke?" Ten added as Luke walked in and sat down.

"Miss who?"

"My point exactly," Ten said.

Nevada looked sharply at his brother, saw only the top of a black head bent over a plateful of excellent food, and muttered something too low for Carla, Mariah or Diana to overhear.

A muffled cry came from the next room. Diana and Carla looked at each other as both pushed back from the table.

"Sit down, Diana," Nevada said. "I'll see what's bothering Carolina. Whatever it is isn't serious. You can tell by her cry."

Both Diana and Carla settled back into their chairs. Neither woman questioned Nevada's words, for they had quickly discovered that he had an uncanny ability to judge not only the identity of a child by its cry but also the urgency of the problem.

"Thanks," Diana said to Nevada's retreating back. Then, softly, she said to Ten, "Your brother is wasted as an uncle. He should have babies of his own to love."

Beneath the table Ten squeezed Diana's hand and said in a low voice, "Nevada's been through too many wars, honey. He doesn't trust life enough to risk loving a woman. And without love, there won't be any babies. The Blackthorns may be the bastard branch of the MacKenzie family, but we don't make babies with women we don't love." His thumb stroked over Diana's palm as he added wryly, "It just took me a while to figure that out in our case."

Diana smiled at Ten and laced her fingers through his.

Nevada's acute hearing had picked up every syllable of the conversation between Diana and her husband. Nevada didn't disagree with Ten's assessment of the Blackthorn clan. The day Nevada had discovered Diana could be pregnant and was definitely alone—because Ten was uncertain of his own ability to love—Nevada had taken his brother out to a lonely stretch of pasture and given him the fight Ten had been begging for since the day Diana had left the Rocking M.

It had been a learning experience for both men. One of the things they had learned was that the love of a brother for a brother was a lot deeper than either had suspected.

"Well, little lady," Nevada said, bending down over Carolina's playpen and lifting her into his arms. "You're as fat and sassy as a summer storm. You want to cloud up and rain all over me?"

Carolina had no such intention now that one of her favorite human beings was within reach. She made a cooing, crowing sound of triumph and grabbed Nevada's beard. He endured the rough caress for a time before gently disengaging her small, surprisingly strong fingers.

"Easy does it," he murmured, rubbing his beard against Carolina's small hands and cheeks. "You'll have me bald before you're a year old."

She laughed with delight and grabbed for the intriguing chin fur again. Nevada blew on Carolina's head teasingly, stirring her silky black hair, the legacy of her Blackthorn father. Her eyes were Diana's—a dark, astonishingly clear blue. Carolina's smile was unique, a smile like sunrise, a contagion of warmth. Holding Carolina, turning his shoulders slowly from side to side, Nevada spoke softly.

"Just lonely, huh?" Nevada murmured, his deep voice gentle, almost a purr. "Well, don't you worry, little darling. Logan's almost over the flu. In a few days he'll be back to stealing your toys. For now, though, he's out of commission. Guess you'll have to settle for me tonight. But your 'uncle' Cash should be back from Boulder by the weekend. He's an even bigger sucker for little girls than I am."

Carolina cooed. Thick black eyelashes swept down over brilliant blue eyes. She curled up against Nevada's chest, yawned, rubbed her ear with a small fist, and relaxed completely. Thirty seconds later she was asleep.

Nevada stood for a long time, cradling the little girl's head with his hand, rocking her very gently, remembering too many babies who had been born into a war-torn land, babies too weak even to cry out, babies he had found too late....

"You're going to spoil her," Ten said from the doorway, but his smile was as affectionate as his voice.

"My pleasure," Nevada said, looking down at his sleeping niece. "She's such a healthy, pretty little thing. Your hair and Diana's eyes."

"And your smile," Ten said softly. "But Luke and I are the only ones who know about that. We're the only ones who remember you from the time before you gave up smiling."

Nevada shrugged slightly. "That's what happens when you wrestle with the devil and lose."

"Is it? I wrestled. I lost. And I learned to smile again anyway."

"Then you're a fool, Tennessee. Any man who lets emotions affect him is a fool."

"Any man who doesn't is dead in all the ways that matter, and you damn well know it. That's why you're standing there holding Carolina."

"She's hardly more than a baby. She needs to be held, needs to know she's not alone, needs..." Nevada shrugged again. "She needs holding, that's all."

"So do adults. Sometimes we need it most of all."

"At over six feet, you're a little big for cuddling," Nevada said dryly.

"Don't tell that to the Rocking M women," Ten retorted. "Luke, Cash and I would hate like hell to give up our ration of cuddling!"

Carolina stirred, complained sleepily and burrowed closer to Nevada.

Ten looked at his watch. "Bedtime. Hand her over to Daddy."

Nevada shifted Carolina into her father's arms. She opened her eyes, approved her new transportation, and promptly went back to sleep. Ten kissed the silky black hair and headed for the stairway.

"Ten?"

"Yeah?" Ten asked softly without looking back.

"If you're sure you don't need me around here, I think I'll head for Wildfire Canyon early tomorrow."

"Happy hunting."

Only Carolina could have seen Ten's wide, knowing smile, and she was asleep.

"Would you miss one of the ranch trucks?" Nevada continued. "We—I lost the cat's tracks on a windy slope way back up a canyon. Even a dog couldn't track her there. It's too steep for a horse, so I might as well drive up that old logging road and work back down from there."

"Take the black truck. Take extra supplies. Take anything you need to get the job done right, including time. For once we're not shorthanded. In other words, don't hurry back."

Sensing the buried amusement in Ten's voice, Nevada watched closely as his brother disappeared up the stairway, carrying the utterly relaxed child.

Abruptly Nevada turned away and went to the bunkhouse. He packed what he would need, set his mental alarm clock for five hours of sleep and crawled into his cold bunk, trying not to remember what it had been like to hold Eden for just a few moments in his arms in an isolated cabin when she had been disturbed by his dark, unremembered dreams.

Nevada slept quickly, deeply, and he did not remember his dreams. Five hours later he awakened, dressed, and went to the black pickup truck. When he opened the door, a mélange of fragrances greeted him—Carla's chocolate chip cookies and Mariah's fudge brownies, a sack of freshly baked biscuits and a kettle of hearty beef stew that would feed him for several days.

The corner of Nevada's mouth turned up as Ten's words came back to him: *Don't tell that to the Rocking M women. Luke, Cash and I would hate like hell to give up our ration of cuddling!*

Something told Nevada that the women enjoyed it, too.

By the time Nevada had negotiated the final washout on the abandoned logging road, he was beginning to wonder how Eden had managed the trip in the first place. If it hadn't been for the signs of her vehicle tracks, he would have sworn that no one had been over the road since the logging operation had been shut down a decade ago. In an emergency, it would be impossible to get to the cabin quickly—or to get away from it.

The anxiety that had been gnawing at Nevada ever since he had left Eden increased as the truck bumped and labored over the rutted, slushy track. He told himself there was no reason for him to be concerned about Eden's welfare. There had been no new storms, no word of strangers in the high country, nothing to set his mind to worrying. Even if there had been, Baby was a formidable bodyguard and Eden had been very much at home in the wild. Rationally, Nevada knew he didn't need to worry about her.

But he wasn't feeling very rational at the moment.

Eden haunted him like an echo down a lonely canyon, touching hidden places that even the sun couldn't reach. Nevada knew he wouldn't have any peace of mind until he assured himself that Eden was all right.

Impatient with himself for his own foolishness, Nevada braked to a stop in front of the isolated cabin. Beyond the cabin, the open, sparse forest began. Even before he turned off the engine, the anxiety that had been driving him intensified. There was smoke rising from the chimney but no one was coming out to greet him. Light green eyes noted every detail of the cabin. Though the weather had been clear, the only tracks Nevada could see in the melting snow went from the cabin around to the outhouse in back, with a single set of tracks detouring to the woodpile.

Eden hadn't left the cabin for anything but absolute necessities.

I knew it. Damn it, I never should have left her alone. Accidents happen. Hell, one happened to me!

Nevada left the truck and reached the cabin door in three long strides. He opened the door and automatically shut it behind him. Baby whined and rumbled a greeting.

"Hi," Eden said, then coughed before continuing in a raspy voice. "Baby told me company was coming, but he didn't say who."

Dressed in the long, scarlet ski underwear she used as pajamas, Eden was kneeling in front of the hearth, raking up the coals of last night's fire. Her hair was tangled and her normally luminous skin was the color of chalk except for the fever flags flying across her high cheekbones. With less than her usual ease, Eden pushed herself slowly to her feet.

"Sit down," she said, gesturing toward a camp chair. "It will be a few minutes until the coffee is ready."

"You're sick," Nevada said flatly, starting toward her.

"It's just—"

Eden's explanation ended in a startled sound as Nevada lifted her off her feet and returned her to her mattress and bedding without so much as a word of warning. Gently, implacably, he stuffed her under the covers. Against the dullness of her skin, her eyes appeared unnaturally brilliant.

"Nevada, what—"

Again Eden's words ended in a startled sound. Nevada's hands were beneath her ears, moving below her chin line and down her neck, probing gently, checking for swollen glands.

"Tender?" he asked curtly.

Wordlessly Eden shook her head. Nevada's eyes were so close, so intent, so beautiful in their concern. Her breath came in raggedly and she shivered at the feel of his hands touching her. Two long, elegantly masculine fingers settled over the pulse in her throat and pressed gently.

"Strong but much too fast," Nevada said.

Eden remembered taking Nevada's pulse and feeling it accelerate at her touch. She smiled crookedly and began to give his words back to him.

"If you were a woman—" she began.

"I'm not," he cut in.

"Yes. Definitely. There's a direct correlation between your masculinity and my pulse rate."

For a moment Eden would have sworn that Nevada was surprised. If he was, he recovered instantly.

"Feeling sassy, are we?" he asked in a dry voice.

"I can't speak for you, but in my case any sassiness is temporary."

"I'm glad you realize it. If your temperature isn't about a hundred and two, I'll eat that bedroll."

Eden let out a shaky breath. "Please don't. Even with Baby as a bunkmate I'd get awfully cold."

At the sound of his name, Baby came over, stuck his outrageously cold nose against Eden's neck and whimpered softly. She lifted her hands and rubbed the wolf's big head. Nevada felt a chill condense along his spine when he saw the trembling of her fingers. The pressure of her hands barely dented the wolf's thick fur.

"Damn it, Eden, you're as weak as a baby."

Eyes closed, she shook her head and smiled in Nevada's general direction. "It's just flu. I've survived much worse."

"Not when you were living alone in a cold cabin at the butt end of nowhere," Nevada said harshly.

"Wrong," she said, sighing, no longer fighting her exhaustion. "The last time I was sick I was living in a Yukon cabin that could teach cold to a glacier.''

"What?"

"Mom and Dad were Alaskan homesteaders who believed in doing things the hard way.''

"They left you alone when you were sick?'' Nevada asked in disbelief.

"Dad was working the trap line and Mom was helping Mrs. Thompson with her new baby. Besides, it was just a cold and Mark was there, too. Then Mark's ski-doo went through the river ice in front of the cabin...."

Eden's voice faded into a yawn. When she spoke again Nevada had to lean down to hear her slow words.

"By the time I helped him home...got his arm splinted... We were pretty sorry puppies for a day or two." She yawned again. "But we made it just fine."

"Splinted his arm?" Nevada asked.

Eden mumbled something that Nevada couldn't understand. Then she shivered and rolled onto her side, wrapping covers around herself.

With a few quick movements Nevada peeled off his heavy shearling coat and put it over her. Then he went to work on the fire. A few minutes later burnished orange flames leaped above the wood, sending heat into the room. With the competence of a man who has spent a lot of time cooking over open fires, Nevada went to work putting together a rich soup.

When Nevada turned back to Eden, she had drifted into a feverish sleep. Frowning, Nevada sat on his heels next to her, watching her intently. Though Eden's skin and lips were dry, she showed no sign of real dehydration. And while her color was chalky, it had none of the ash-gray or yellow tones of serious illness.

When Nevada put his palm on Eden's forehead, she made a murmurous sound and turned toward him as though seeking more of his touch.

Baby whined and nudged his mistress.

"She'll be all right," Nevada said, gently pushing the wolf's long, narrow muzzle away from Eden's cheek. "Let her sleep while I bring in the rest of the supplies. She won't be hungry when I wake her up, but she'll eat."

Eden slept on while Nevada came and went, emptying the truck and filling the cabin with the fragrance of food. She stirred several times when the sharp sounds of an ax striking wood came through the cabin's log walls, but she didn't awaken until Nevada pulled her half-upright across his lap, propped her against his chest and held a steaming mug of soup under her nose.

"Wake up, Sleeping Beauty."

"Not . . . beautiful," she mumbled.

Nevada disagreed, but he did it silently. "It's just as well, honey. I'm no genteel prince with a magic kiss for you."

Eden grumbled sleepily about being disturbed, yet even as she complained she turned and snuggled against Nevada, trusting him as completely as Carolina had. Without intending to, Nevada found himself setting the soup aside and holding Eden close while one big hand smoothed over her hair and forehead and cheek. He told himself that he was simply seeing if her temperature had dropped, but he didn't believe it. Nevada had never been very good at lying to himself.

"If you're not Sleeping Beauty," he said in a deep voice, "you must be Little Red Riding Hood. Wake up, Red."

Long, sable eyelashes stirred. Eyes that were green and gold and blue and gray, the color of every season, looked up at Nevada.

"You don't look like my grandmother."

"That's because I'm the wolf."

"Goody," Eden sighed, smiling and rubbing her cheek against Nevada's bearded jaw. "I've always had a weakness for furry beasts."

"The weakness is in your head," he retorted, his voice both hard and deep. He forced himself to turn away from the vulnerable spot just behind Eden's ear. "Furry beasts always have sharp teeth to use on tempting little morsels like you."

"Sounds exciting," she said, yawning. Then she made a sound of contentment and let her weight rest fully against Nevada. "Know something? You're much more comfortable than my mattress."

Eden smiled dreamily and curled more deeply into Nevada's lap. As she moved against him, the sleeping bag, extra blankets and coat slid off her shoulders, revealing the firm, curving lines of her breasts against the deep red of her ski underwear. When the chilly air seeped through red cloth, her nipples tightened.

Nevada's heartbeat hesitated for an instant before it resumed at a harder, quicker rate.

"Damn it, Eden, *sit up.*"

"Sheesh . . . what a grouch."

Eden's attempts to sit up involved bracing herself against Nevada. Fever and sleepiness made her clumsy. Her hands slipped and fumbled down the length of his torso before coming to rest on his hard thighs. Even harder male flesh rose insistently only a fraction of an inch away from her right hand.

Nevada closed his eyes and told himself he was glad that Eden's hand hadn't come to rest a fraction of an inch to the left. He didn't believe that lie, either.

Slim fingers braced themselves on the clenched power of Nevada's thighs, but he sensed that Eden's balance was still uncertain, that her hands were sliding . . .

Abruptly Eden felt herself being lifted off Nevada's lap. Strong hands wrapped the shearling coat firmly around her and buttoned it, imprisoning her arms against her body.

"Warm enough?" Nevada asked through his teeth.

She nodded.

"Good." He grabbed the mug of warm soup. "Open your mouth."

She opened her mouth.

"Drink."

She drank, swallowed, licked her lips and said, "Nevada, what's wrong?"

"Drink."

Silently Eden drank from the mug that Nevada was holding against her mouth. When she finished the soup, she tried to lick the creamy mustache from her upper lip, couldn't reach all of it, and tried again.

Nevada closed his eyes and said something harsh beneath his breath.

"So I'm a little messy," Eden muttered. "What do you expect? I'm not used to being fed. If you'll let me out of this straitjacket I'll feed myself."

Nevada came to his feet in a tightly coordinated rush, stalked to the fire, ladled out another mug of soup and went back to Eden. His jacket was so big on her that she had managed to get her arms through the sleeves even though she was buttoned inside.

And now she was watching him with eyes whose color shifted at each leap of flame. She hadn't a third of his strength, she wasn't two-thirds of his weight, yet she was utterly calm. She trusted him with an unshakable certainty that was as arousing as it was infuriating.

"You just don't get it, do you?" Nevada asked tightly.

"Get what?"

"You're so damned vulnerable," he said, "and too damned sexy. I mean it, Eden. *Don't trust me.*"

She started to speak, looked at his bleak eyes, and shivered. But it wasn't fear that made her tremble, nor was it cold. It was the realization that Nevada was watching her the way a wild animal watches a winter campfire, both lured by and deeply wary of the dancing warmth, easing closer and closer only to snarl and spring back and circle once more, watching what it wants but is too wild and wary to take, watching her with eyes as cold as winter itself.

"I can no more help trusting you than you can help wanting me," Eden said finally. "I'm not nearly as fragile as you seem to think. And ... and you must know that I want to touch you, too, Nevada. I'm not very good at hiding how I feel."

Eden watched the centers of Nevada's eyes expand, saw the sudden rush of blood in the pulse beating rapidly at his temple, and cleared her throat.

"May I have some more soup, please?" she asked in a trembling voice. "It's...it's very good."

With great care Nevada placed the mug in Eden's outstretched hand, stood up and walked out of the cabin.

8

The first red-gold tint of dawn had barely seeped through the cabin window when Baby scratched at the door, looked toward Eden's sleeping bag, then pawed the door again.

"Lord, Baby," Eden muttered, sitting up, yawning. "Don't you ever sleep?"

Baby whined.

"Stay put," said a deep voice. "I'll let him out."

Eden looked over at the mound of sleeping bag and blankets that was Nevada. "I'm already up. Besides, I've done nothing but lie around since you got here three days ago." She rubbed her eyes and stretched again. "I'm like Baby—ready to prowl."

Nevada didn't bother to argue. He came out of the sleeping bag and got to his feet in an uninterrupted motion, took two long strides and opened the cabin door. Baby flowed outside like a shadow left over from the vanishing night. Nevada shut the door and turned back toward his sleeping bag.

Eden's breath came in with an audible rush when she opened her eyes once more. Nevada wore only black jeans, and all but one of the steel buttons were undone. Hints of golden light caressed him like a lover, emphasizing the shift and coil of powerful muscles beneath smooth skin. Black hair glowed and licked over his torso like dark flames. An odd feeling lanced through Eden, a hunger and a yearning that was unlike anything she had ever experienced.

When Nevada reached for his black flannel shirt and began putting it on, Eden wanted to protest. She also wanted to run her hands over Nevada, to test the strength and resilience of his muscles, to savor all the textures of his midnight hair with her palms and fingertips, to taste his lips, his cheeks, his eyelashes, his shoulders, to trace every velvet shadow on his body with the tip of her tongue....

"Eden? Are you all right?" Nevada stared into the shadows, wondering at the cause of Eden's unnatural stillness.

"Yes," she said faintly.

"You don't sound like it," he said as he rolled up his sleeves. "How does your chest feel? Still tight?"

"I'm fine."

"You won't be if you don't stay warm." Nevada crossed the cabin, knelt, and stuffed Eden back under the mound of covers. "You're shivering. Damn it, are you trying to get pneumonia?"

Eden shook her head. "Don't worry. I'm a long way from pneumonia."

"I knew you believed in fairy tales," he muttered, pulling the blankets up to Eden's chin. "Pneumonia is unpredictable. One minute you've got the flu or a cold and the next minute, *bang,* you're fighting for your life."

Memories sleeted through Eden, ripping away everything but the past. She tried to speak but had no voice. She swallowed and tried again.

"I know about pneumonia."

The resonances of certainty, grief and acceptance in Eden's voice made Nevada's hands pause over her blankets. He looked at her intently. In the increasing light of dawn her eyes were wide, shimmering with tears, unblinking, focused on something only she could see.

He caught a tear on his fingertip. It burned against his skin like a molten diamond.

"Eden," he said softly.

She let out her breath in a ragged sigh and blinked away the tears. "It's all right. It's just that sometimes...sometimes the memories...are stronger than other times."

"Yes," he said simply. "Sometimes they are."

Hazel eyes focused on Nevada. Eden smiled despite the traces of tears still shining on her eyelashes.

"The memories aren't sad, not completely," she said. "Just . . . bittersweet. Aurora was ten months old, and alive the way only a healthy baby can be. Tears and laughter, going full tilt one minute and sound asleep the next. Sweet little tornado. Her laughter made me think of bright orange poppies."

Eden smiled, remembering, and her smile was as real as her tears had been. Nevada's throat tightened around emotions he had not permitted himself to feel for too many years.

"How long ago," he asked, his voice low.

"Six years. Early in spring. I was sixteen, too old to be a child and not old enough to be anything else," Eden said, looking past Nevada, remembering another time, another place. "My sister, Aurora, was almost one. She got sick the way babies do, sniffles and short temper and endless fussing. Then she got an ear infection, then another cold, another infection, a cough, and each time she fussed less."

Eden hesitated before continuing in a low voice. "A late storm came down out of the Arctic, the temperature dropped seventy degrees and Aurora's breathing changed. We managed to get out on the radio to ask for help, but nothing could fly in that storm. All we could do was keep Aurora warm and pray that the storm broke in time.''

Nevada closed his eyes for a moment, understanding all too well the feelings of helplessness and pain that Eden's family had endured. He had seen too many shattered families, shattered villages, shattered lands.

"I was the only one who didn't have a cold," Eden continued in a low voice, "so Aurora was sleeping with me. I was holding her when she died. I held her ... for a long time."

The only sound was that of Nevada's big hands smoothing the blankets around Eden's shoulders as he watched her with an intensity that was almost tangible. He had no doubt of the depth and power of her grief. He could feel it beating silently around him, black velvet wings of sorrow and loss.

But he also had seen Eden smile, heard her laugh—and that, too, was genuine. Her joy in life was vivid and complex, generous and oddly serene. That was what had drawn him instantly to her—his absolute certainty that life was a hot golden cataract flowing through Eden, a fire that would burn against any darkness, any ice, any night.

Eden still smiled, although she knew that life was cruel and unpredictable, knew that it had betrayed joy and trust, leaving her to hold a dying child in her arms. She was even able to laugh.

"The ring on your necklace. It belonged to Aurora."

There was no question in Nevada's deep voice, but Eden answered anyway.

"Yes."

"Why."

Again it was not a question, not quite a plea, not fully a demand. Again Eden softly answered.

"I wear Aurora's ring to remind myself that love is never wasted, never futile."

Something stirred deep within Nevada, a part of him so long hidden that he believed it had died. The pain that came was shocking, making it impossible to breathe, much less to speak.

And he wanted to speak. He wanted to argue with Eden. He wanted it so fiercely that his hands clenched on the blankets. Yet he could find no words to counter Eden's certainty, no words to shake her serenity, nothing to equal her laughter; only a bleak, incoherent cry clawing at his soul, a cry of rage or fear or hope . . . or a wrenching blend of all three.

In a rush of barely controlled power, Nevada stood up and turned away from Eden. Silently she watched while he stirred the banked fire into life with a few harsh strokes, added wood, and walked to the sink. He dipped water from the bucket, primed the pump, and worked the long iron handle as savagely as though he were killing snakes.

Water sped up from the hidden well and leaped out of the pump in a rushing crystal stream.

He filled three buckets, a kettle and the coffeepot before he released the pump handle. Buckets and kettle went to the hearth. The coffeepot went on the single-burner backpacking stove Eden had brought. Each move Nevada made was controlled, graceful despite the anger radiating from him like heat from the hearth.

Eden watched Nevada, reminded of the first cougar she had ever seen. It had been caged, and wild within that cage, raking with unsheathed claws at everything that came near.

What is it, Nevada? What did I say to make you so angry?

The question was asked only in the silence of Eden's mind, for she knew Nevada wouldn't answer if she spoke aloud.

After a few minutes Eden groped around in her sleeping bag, found her clothes, and dressed within the cocoon of blankets and bag. Even with pre-warmed jeans and a turtleneck sweater, she shivered when she crawled out into the cold air of the cabin. She pushed her stockinged feet into her fleece-lined moccasins, pulled on her jacket and went outside.

The soft closing of the door was like a gunshot in the taut silence of the cabin. Nevada put one more piece of firewood on the flames and sat on his heels in front of the hearth, watching the renewed leap of fire with bleak green eyes. But it wasn't the flames he was seeing. It was Eden's tears, Eden's smile, Eden's lips, Eden's eyes admiring him, wanting him.

Nevada spread his hands before the fire, saw their fine trembling, and balled his fingers into fists. He wanted Eden. He wanted her until he shook with it.

A raw word tore through the silence.

"Other than that, how do you feel?" Eden asked dryly, closing the door behind her.

Nevada spun around and came to his feet with shocking speed, his body poised for defense or attack. He hadn't heard Eden open the door.

He hadn't heard her.

"I must be losing my edge," Nevada said, lowering his hands.

She shrugged and hung her jacket on a nearby nail. "More likely your subconscious figured out I'm no threat to you, so why spend energy staying on guard?"

"No threat," Nevada repeated. Abruptly he had an impulse to laugh that was more shocking to him than the fact that he had been too caught up in his own thoughts to hear the cabin door opening behind him. "Lady, the only threat that matters is the one you don't see coming. That's the one that gets you."

"I'm not big enough to 'get' you." Eden looked past Nevada. "Besides, you can read my mind."

"I can?"

"The buckets."

"What?" he asked, taken off guard once more. Nevada turned and looked at the buckets warming next to the fire as though he had never seen them. In some ways it was true. He had pumped water as a physical outlet, not because they needed three buckets plus a kettle of water warming by the fire. "The buckets make me a mind reader?"

"Sure. You knew I wanted to take a bath. Presto. Bathwater appears."

"Wrong. You're not well enough yet."

"Pucky."

Nevada blinked. "What?"

"Don't try to change the subject. I need a bath. This time you're not going to talk me out of it."

"I didn't talk you out of it last time," Nevada pointed out coolly. "I just said I wasn't going anywhere and you decided not to have a bath after all."

"Um. Well, this time you won't get away with it. If I don't wash my hair it's going to get up and walk off my head."

"Eden—" Nevada began.

"Nope," she interrupted. "No deal. I haven't run a fever for almost two days. I'm having a bath and that's all there is to it."

"What if I stay and watch?"

"I'll blush a lot, but I'll survive."

"You're playing with fire," he said flatly.

"People who are cold tend to do that."

Nevada shook his head in disbelief, hardly able to comprehend that someone as soft and vulnerable as Eden was ignoring the kind of warnings that had made grown men back off. "Has anyone ever mentioned that you're too stubborn for your own good?"

"Frequently. Gives me great faith in the powers of human observation."

Narrowed green eyes swept over Eden's slender body. "Oh, I'm an observant, noticing kind of man, as you pointed out. Right now I'm noticing how hard and tight your nipples get when they're cold. Do they get like that for a man's mouth, too?"

Eden's lips opened but no sound came out. She was too surprised to think coherently, much less speak.

"I've noticed your tongue, too," Nevada continued. "Quick and pink and clever. I'd like to feel it all over, everywhere, every last damned aching inch of me. But most of all I've noticed those long, long legs of yours. I want to be where they meet. I want to sink into you, all the way in, and I want to watch you while I do it. I want it so much I wake up sweating." His pale, crystalline eyes pinned Eden. "Still planning on taking a bath in front of me?"

"You're not—you can't—damn it, Nevada, you won't—"

Nevada hooked his thumbs in his belt loops and waited, watching Eden with eyes that missed nothing and concealed nothing of his response to what he saw.

Eden said something succinct and inelegant, glared at Nevada and stalked past him to the fire. Calmly Nevada joined her and added more wood, redoubling the flames.

"Scrambled eggs or oatmeal?" he asked as though nothing had happened.

"No," she said between her teeth. "Thank you."

"So polite."

"You ought to try it sometime. Works wonders in human relationships."

"I prefer honesty."

"Do you? Then try this." She flashed him a sideways look from brilliant hazel eyes. "I'm not angry because you want me. I'm angry because you *hate* wanting me. Why, Nevada? What is so awful about wanting me?"

"Not having you."

The breath, and much of the anger, went out of Eden in a long sigh. She started to speak, made a helpless gesture of appeal with her hands, and tried again.

"I won't say no to you, Nevada."

"Why? Do you go to bed with every man who wants you?"

"What do you think?"

"I think you're damned fussy about who touches you."

"I think you're right."

"So why me, Eden?"

When Eden opened her mouth to explain the complex, unexpected, seething, surprising mixture of emotions Nevada called out of her, the only words she could think of were very simple.

"I love you, Nevada."

His mouth flattened into a savage line. "That's what I was afraid you were telling yourself. Fairy tales. You can't accept that all there is between us is sex. I wanted you the instant I saw you. You wanted me the same way. Calling it love doesn't change what it is. Sex. Pure and simple and hot as hell."

"You can call it whatever you want."

"But you'll call it love, right?"

"Why do you care what I call it? I'm not asking you to lie to me about how you feel. When you get right down to it, I've never asked you for one damn thing but a bath!"

Nevada kept on talking as though Eden had never spoken. "Let me tell you what the real world is like, fairy-tale girl. The real world is Afghanistan, where you walk through a narrow mountain pass in single file with five handpicked men and arrive at your destination and look around and you're alone, nothing on your back trail but blood and silence. The real world is a place where you fight for what you believe in, and then find out that win or lose, the weak and helpless are still the first to die. The real world is a place where you know a hundred ways to kill a man and not one damned way to save a baby's life.''

Eden tried to speak. It was futile. Nevada kept on talking, his eyes like splinters of ice, his voice emotionless, his words relentless, hammering on her, forcing her to hear.

"The real world is a place where you walk into villages with men whose wives and sisters and mothers and daughters have been murdered in ways you can't even imagine, villages where children are diseased and maimed by starvation, villages where babies are too weak to cry because they starved in the womb and their mothers have no milk and by the time you get to them, all you can do with your prayers and medicine and rage is hold those babies until they die and then you bury them and walk away, *just walk away,* because any man who cares for anything enough to be hurt by its loss is a fool.''

"Nevada," Eden whispered, reaching for him, wanting to comfort him. "Nevada, I—"

Her words ended with a startled sound when his hands flashed out and pinned her wrists against her sides.

"Don't touch me, Eden," Nevada said in a low voice, but even as he spoke he was leaning down, coming closer to her, so close that all that lay between their mouths was the mingled heat of their breath. "I want you too much. I want you until I can't sleep, can't take a deep breath, can't look at my hands without seeing them on your body, can't—my God, I can't even lick my lips without wondering what you would taste like."

"Find out," Eden whispered against his lips. "Taste me, Nevada."

With a sound that was almost anguished, Nevada lowered his head the final fraction of an inch.

Eden's lips were soft, warm, undefended. They opened for Nevada without hesitation, yielding the secrets of her mouth to him at the first gliding touch of his tongue. Hot, generous, sweet, clean—he could not get enough of her. The changing taste and texture of her mouth lured him deeper and deeper until he could go no farther and yet he still wanted more, so much more. He was straining against her, shaking, tormented by all that he would not allow himself to take.

Then he realized that Eden was trembling, too, and her tears were hot against his lips. He tore his mouth from hers and stepped back, releasing her wrists as though they had burned him. When he licked his lips he tasted the salt of her tears. Something deep within him ached with a surprising pain.

He had tried to stay away from Eden because he had known that all he had to give her was tears. What he hadn't known was that he could still feel pain himself. The realization shocked him.

"Do you understand now?" Nevada asked in a soft voice, but there was nothing of softness in his eyes, his body, his certainty, his memories.

Eden was too shaken by Nevada's passion and his pain to do more than nod her head. At that instant she knew how he felt beyond any doubt or wishful misunderstanding. Her instincts had been right. Nevada was a winter man, his emotions frozen, and he was that way by choice, not accident. He had been stretched to the breaking point in Afghanistan. He had not broken.

And the price of remaining sane had been to walk away from his emotions. They were a weakness in a time and place where only the strongest and most fierce survived. Nevada Blackthorn had survived.

Warrior.

Eden had spoken only in the silence of her mind, yet Nevada's expression changed. He knew her too well, had known her instantly and wanted her with a violence equaled only by his refusal to acknowledge the possibility of love.

Sex, not love, Eden reminded herself, understanding now why Nevada had insisted on making the distinction ruthlessly clear.

Fairy tales. Fairy-tale girl.

Eyes closed, Eden interlaced her fingers to keep from reaching for Nevada in an offer of comfort and healing that he neither wanted nor would permit. Yet somehow she had to free her beautiful trapped cougar without getting ripped to pieces in the process.

If she could free him at all.

There was no guarantee of success. There was just his need and her love and the battle yet to be fought.

Win, lose or draw, she told herself bracingly.

No. It's win or lose, period. Nevada doesn't know any other way.

No second place. No truce. No genteel neutral ground between victory or defeat where two people could meet and shake hands and talk politely about things that didn't matter. Either they both won or they both lost. Whatever the outcome, Nevada would discover that he wasn't the only one willing to fight for what he believed in.

And what Eden believed in was love.

"Coffee's ready. Want some?" Nevada asked.

"Please," Eden said absently, still caught in the instant she had first understood the risk and necessity of what she must do.

"Back to being polite, huh?" he asked. He crouched over the coffeepot and poured a fragrant stream of coffee into a mug.

Eden gave Nevada a sidelong glance from her place by the hearth and decided it was time to fire the opening shot of her undeclared war.

"Go to the devil, Nevada, but hand over my coffee first."

His mouth lifted at the left corner. Without looking at Eden he set the pot back on the burner and handed her the mug as he turned back to the fire.

"Guess I had that one coming," he said.

"And a few more besides. But I'm feeling generous."

Nevada turned and looked at Eden over his shoulder. "That was the second thing I noticed about you in West Fork. Your smile. Not a bit of calculation in it. Generous."

"My smile was the second thing, huh? So what was the first thing you noticed?"

"I'm a man," Nevada said dryly. "What do you think I noticed?"

"That I was wearing a quilted down jacket?" Eden suggested, her voice as dry as his.

"Yeah, something like that. Then you started walking. You move like a woman."

"Nevada, I *am* a woman."

He shot Eden a glittering green look before he turned back to the fire. "You were the wrong woman in the wrong place at the wrong time—and you walked right up to me."

"You had a beard."

"So did the bartender."

"I liked yours better. It looked sleek and healthy, a wonderful male pelt. I wanted to rub my cheek against it to see if it felt as good as it looked." Eden set aside the coffee mug, stretched and smiled to herself as she fired the second shot. "Then I found out it felt even better than it looked. When you kissed me, your beard was like a thick silk brush on my skin. I liked that, Nevada. It made me wonder what your beard would feel like on my neck, on my bare shoulders, on the inside of my wrists, between my—"

"You just can't stop pushing, can you?" Nevada interrupted roughly.

Eden finished stretching, lowered her arms, and let her fingertips idly brush Nevada's hair. "When you don't leave me any room to move, it's hard not to push."

Nevada hesitated in the act of dropping another piece of wood on the already vigorous fire. When he let go of the wood, there was a shower of sparks. Without a word he rotated the buckets, bringing a cool side to meet the increasing heat of the flames.

He stretched out a long arm, picked up the mug of coffee and handed it to Eden again.

"Nervous?" he asked dryly.

"What?"

"You're petting me. That's what you do when you're nervous, isn't it? Pet the nearest thing?"

Eden realized that her fingertips had returned to ruffling Nevada's hair as though he were Baby. "Like I said. It's hard not to push or touch when you're being crowded."

"I didn't know I was crowding you," Nevada said, pinning her with a pale green glance. "In fact, I would have sworn it was the other way around."

For a moment Eden sipped coffee, gathering her scattered thoughts. She had fired the first two shots, yet she felt as though she had just stumbled into an ambush. The combination of passion and calculation in Nevada's eyes was unnerving. Obviously there was more to this kind of skirmish than she had thought. Maybe she would be better off doing as Nevada did—using the kind of honesty that could rock a man back on his heels.

"I'm not used to being told when I can track cats," Eden said, "or when I can take a bath, what I can eat, where I can—"

"You're sick," Nevada interrupted.

"I was sick. I'm well now. I have a very good appreciation of my own physical limits. Being raised in the Yukon does that for you. I'm fine,

Nevada. So if you keep me locked up any longer, you'd better be prepared to deal with a major case of the rips."

"The rips?"

"Yeah. I'm like Baby. If I can't tear around outside, I'll tear around inside."

"The rips," Nevada repeated, shaking his head. "Honey, I've never met anyone like you."

"That makes us even," Eden said, watching him over the rim of the mug. "I've never met anyone like you, either. And I've never been kissed like that, heaven and hell and the rainbow burning between..."

She saw the sudden expansion of Nevada's pupils, heard the intake of his breath, sensed the hot leap of his blood.

"Was it like that for you, Nevada?"

For an electric instant Eden thought Nevada was going to pull her down to the hearth and kiss her again. Instead, he came to his feet in a lithe rush, stalked across the cabin, grabbed his jacket and opened the front door.

"I'm going to look for that cougar's den."

"Too much honesty, huh?" asked Eden. "Want me to go back to being polite? Or would you rather I just work off my excess energy by petting you?"

The door closed very softly behind Nevada.

"If Baby gets in your way, send him back to me," Eden called through the door. "I'll frolic with him, instead."

Nevada didn't answer.

Eden went to the window and looked out. Nevada was heading across the clearing with long, determined strides. An ecstatic Baby was leaping around him.

"I think, in military terminology, Nevada just executed a strategic disengagement," Eden said aloud. "Ordinary folks would call it a retreat."

Smiling, she tested the water in the nearest bucket and nodded approvingly. By the time she finished breakfast, the water would be warm enough for a bath.

Two hours later Eden was humming softly, feeling as clean as the sunlight itself. When she went outside to check on the bedding she had draped over the woodpile to air, warm air surrounded her. She shook out Nevada's sleeping bag and flipped it over to soak up more sunshine. The sheet she used to line her own bag was hanging from a rope strung between the cabin and a nearby tree. She touched the sheet. Nearly dry, but not quite. The lacy beige bras were still damp. The pairs of panties were almost dry, but not quite. She decided she could live without underwear for another hour. She went to check on her own bag, which was thrown over a bush in the clearing beyond the cabin. Warm air was everywhere, breathing spring into the day.

With the season's typical capriciousness, a chinook had arrived, sending the temperature soaring into the seventies. Meltwater trickled and glittered and shone everywhere. The sunlight itself was hot. The shade was crisp. The warm wind was a transparent river of wine. The air was rich with the scent of newly revealed earth. Every breath, every instant of being alive, was a sensual feast.

When a hidden bird sang, Eden stopped in the act of reaching for her sleeping bag and closed her eyes, absorbing the piercing, unexpected song with the same intense awareness with which she absorbed the sunlight itself. The bird repeated its call, notes rippling and soaring, transforming the day with music.

There was a rush of air, the near-silent brushing of feet against the ground, and a certainty that she was no longer alone. Eden opened her eyes and turned around.

"Hello, Baby," she said, rubbing the animal's fur, but it was Nevada she was looking at. In the sunlight he looked both dark and fierce, the power of him apparent in even his smallest movement. "Did you find what you were looking for?"

"I narrowed the search area. I'll try again after lunch. With this chinook, the snow is melting fast, even in sheltered places." Nevada's eyes noted the sheen of Eden's pale hair, the delicate color of her cheeks, the subtle radiance of her skin that only health could give. He closed his eyes for an instant, trying to still the hard rush of his blood. It was impossible. "Did you enjoy your bath?"

"Yes. I heated more water for you, in case you were interested."

"I am. Thank you."

Nevada's formality made Eden blink. "You're welcome. Yell when you're finished and I'll make lunch."

Nevada nodded, turned away and walked into the cabin without looking back. Sighing, Eden pulled her sleeping bag off the bush, shook out the warm folds and draped the bag over the bush once more.

Nevada's right. Warfare shouldn't be polite. It's worse that way.

Warfare didn't get any better when conducted over a meal. The hard salami and zesty mustard sandwiches Eden made lost their savor when eaten in stilted silence. She tried conversational gambits that ranged from outrageous to abstruse. Polite, dead-end answers were Nevada's only response.

Finally Eden looked at Baby, who was begging shamelessly at Nevada's knee, and said, "Bite him."

Baby gave his mistress a look of lupine disbelief.

"You heard me," Eden said. "First Nevada complains when I'm polite. Then he walks out on me when I'm honest. Then he uses politeness as a weapon against me. So make lunch out of him. Lord knows the man isn't good for anything else."

Baby ignored her. He rested his long muzzle once again on Nevada's forearm just beneath the rolled-up sleeve.

"Give the man some space, Baby," Eden said. "Can't you see he isn't interested? Quit begging."

Eden winced as her own words echoed in her mind. *Not bad advice. I think I'll take it myself.*

She stood up, opened the cabin door, looked at Baby and said, "Out."

Baby trotted outside, found a pool of deep shade and flopped down. Eden stowed the remaining food in the ice chest and went to stand by the open window, letting sunlight and warm spring wind wash over her.

Nevada finished his sandwich, drank some springwater and began packing his gear and stacking it near the door, ready to be carried to the truck. As the stack grew, Eden realized that Nevada was preparing to return to the ranch headquarters—and there was no guarantee that he would be back at Wildfire Canyon anytime in the future.

The realization sent a chill through Eden. When she had decided to fight the battle on Nevada's terms, she hadn't considered what she would do if he simply withdrew from the field, taking her heart with him and leaving her no chance to touch him in return.

Eden didn't know much about waging war.

Nevada did. He was very good at it.

9

Numbly Eden began stuffing a lightweight down vest and windbreaker into her own backpack.

"Going somewhere?" Nevada asked, watching her intently.

"Cat hunting," Eden said, her voice carefully balanced within her aching throat. "It's something I'm good at. Obviously I'm not good at much else. Kissing, for one. Warfare, for another."

Nevada's eyes narrowed at the sadness Eden couldn't wholly conceal, but all he said was "I'll leave a cellular phone with you. Put it in your backpack."

"No, thank you."

"It isn't a request. It's a Rocking M rule. If you're in the backcountry alone, you carry a cellular phone in case you get into trouble. The coverage isn't perfect, but it's better than nothing."

"It didn't help you last week."

"The phone was in my saddlebag."

"Best place for it."

"Don't be pigheaded," Nevada said impatiently.

"Why not? It works for you."

Eden didn't bother to put on her backpack. She just hooked the straps over her arm as she reached for the front door. She barely had the door open when Nevada's hands shot over her shoulders and slammed the door shut again. His speed was literally breathtaking. The corded power of his bare forearms was a blunt statement of his superior strength. He was a warrior accustomed to fighting—and winning.

"I should let you go," Nevada said, his voice husky. "God help me, I tried to. Then I saw you standing in sunlight listening to a bird sing, and your smile was sad and sweet and so beautiful it damn near brought me to my knees."

Nevada's hands on the door became fists, then slowly relaxed once more, revealing the fine trembling in his fingers.

"Fairy-tale girl, all laughter and golden light," Nevada whispered against Eden. His lips brushed her hair, the curve of her ear, the warmth of her neck. "I'm worlds too hard for you, but I want you until my hands shake."

Silently Eden lifted her own hands, showing their trembling to Nevada. When he saw, he breathed a word that could have been either curse or prayer. She started to turn toward him, only to be pinned against the door by the full length of Nevada's powerful body.

"Think hard before you turn around," he said, his voice rough with the violence of his blood rushing. "I'm not offering you love and happily ever after." Slowly Nevada lowered his head, found the nape of Eden's neck, and bit her with exquisite care. "But when I'm finished, your hands won't be shaking anymore."

Even as the primitive caress shivered through Eden, she found herself freed, no hard masculine torso pinning her, no powerful arms confining her, nothing but the certainty that Nevada was standing barely a hand's breadth away, waiting for her answer. Slowly she let the backpack straps slide from her arm and turned toward him.

The look in Nevada's eyes made Eden's breath stop. With a muffled cry she reached for him even as he reached for her and lifted her, bringing her to his hungry mouth. She slid her arms around his neck and said his name in the instant before his kiss claimed her, taking from her the ability to talk, to think, to breathe.

Eden didn't care. All she wanted was to hold Nevada and to be held by him, to taste him and be tasted in turn, to feel the hardness and restraint of his body against hers. Her fingers smoothed the sleek pelt of his hair and beard before finding his powerful shoulders. Making soft, approving sounds, she kneaded the bunched muscles of his arms, glorying in Nevada's strength even as she gave him her own heat and the sweetness of her mouth in return.

Nevada took everything he wanted from the kiss and discovered that Eden had more to give, much more than he had ever found with any kiss, any woman. Eden's response to him was as loving and generous as summer, a pleasure that increased with each heartbeat, doubling and redoubling until he was focused only in the expanding, timeless instant of the kiss. Urgently he savored Eden's gift, tasting and caressing and enjoying her with slow movements of his tongue, luring her deeper and deeper into passion until her breathing was ragged and her arms were locked around him. Breathing harshly, swiftly, Nevada held on to Eden as though he expected her to be ripped from his arms at any instant.

Finally Nevada lifted his head and let Eden slide down his body, making no attempt to conceal the hard length of his arousal, shuddering openly with pleasure when her hips moved over his as he lowered her feet to the floor. Then he held her tightly, fiercely, while he fought for breath, for control, for the discipline of mind and body that he had learned at such great cost and had taken for granted for so many years.

"My God," Nevada said huskily.

He forced himself to loosen his arms from around Eden. One big hand stroked her hair as he let out his breath in an explosive hiss.

"Nevada?" Eden said, hugging him hard, afraid that he would turn away from her. "What's wrong?"

"Nothing. Everything. You surprised the hell out of me, Eden."

"I did?"

Nevada threaded his fingers through her pale, soft hair, tugging gently backward until Eden's face was turned up to his.

"Yes," he said simply. He caught her lower lip between his teeth, bit gently, and shuddered even as she did. "You wanted me."

Shivering, Eden whispered, "What?"

"I could taste it, feel it, see it. *You wanted me.*"

She watched Nevada with uncertain hazel eyes. "Is that wrong?"

He looked down at her, sensing her confusion as clearly as he had sensed the depth of her passion.

"No, it isn't wrong," Nevada said. "It's just... surprising. No woman has ever kissed me that way. No calculation, nothing held back, just a kiss as hot and honest as fire. Then I was kissing you the same way and you burned even hotter and so did I and it just kept on, hotter and brighter. I could have taken you right there, straight up. God knows I wanted to." A faint tremor rippled through his body. "It was a near thing."

Wide-eyed, still uncertain, Eden watched Nevada, trying to understand.

"You don't get it, do you?" he asked.

She shook her head.

"I didn't come up to Wildfire Canyon expecting to have sex with you," Nevada said bluntly. "In fact, I deliberately emptied out my pockets before I came up here so I wouldn't be tempted to touch you. Well, that didn't work, and now I have no way to keep from getting you pregnant. What about you? Can you protect yourself?"

Eden shook her head again.

Despite the hunger blazing in his eyes, Nevada's mouth kicked up at the left corner. "I didn't think so. You don't sleep with men much, do you?"

For the third time Eden's head moved in a silent negative.

"It's a good thing," he said, bending down to her mouth once more, "that there's more than one way to skin this particular cat."

"What?"

Nevada hesitated, lifted his head enough to see Eden's expression, and asked, "Just how experienced are you, fairy-tale girl?"

She bit her lip and looked at him rather warily. "Are we speaking of practical or intellectual experience?"

"Practical."

"Not much."

"How much is not much?"

"Not. Much."

Nevada whistled softly between his teeth, then said, "You're a virgin, aren't you?"

"That shouldn't matter," Eden said. "Every girl starts out that way."

"My God" was all Nevada could think of to say. He looked at Eden in a combination of disbelief and wonder.

"Don't worry," she said, exasperated. "Virginity isn't contagious."

"I'm not contagious, either," he shot back, "but that's not something you need to worry about."

"I don't understand."

"You're going to stay a virgin."

"But I don't want—"

Nevada kept talking. "You'll be a very experienced sort of virgin, but a virgin just the same."

"What does that mean?"

Nevada's big hands came up, framing Eden's face. He looked from her puzzled hazel eyes to her generous mouth. Her lips were still flushed with the kiss that had taught Nevada more than he thought he had left to learn about men and women and passion. He wondered what else he would learn, what he could teach, what discoveries awaited his exploration of his own private, passionate Eden.

The narrowed green blaze of Nevada's eyes as he watched her mouth made shimmers of sensation curl from Eden's breastbone to her knees. She felt like a tightly furled bud being discovered by the first, searching heat of spring's potent sun.

"Nevada," she whispered. "Aren't you going to kiss me?"

"Do you want to kiss me again?"

"Want?" Eden shivered and laughed softly, almost wildly, wondering how she could make Nevada understand feelings that were so new, so fierce, that she had no names for them. "When I grabbed your wrist to keep you from killing that cowboy in West Fork and you looked at me . . . you *saw* me, Nevada, all the way into me, and then you let me stop you, let me *see* you in return. Nevada," Eden breathed against his lips, standing on tiptoe, "Nevada, I was born for you and you were born for me. I want it all with you, everything, heaven and hell and the rainbow burning between."

With a low sound, Nevada bent and took Eden's mouth, giving her his own in return. When the warmth of her tongue touched his, Nevada's arms tightened, lifting her, bringing her whole body into the embrace. His hips moved slowly against her once, twice, and then he shuddered and eased her down until she was standing on her own feet once more. Holding her tightly, fighting to control his wild response, Nevada tried to end the kiss, but the pleasure of sliding his tongue into Eden's satin sweetness was too great to deny himself.

Just once more. Then I'll stop and catch my breath. Just once...

The hungry, gliding return of Nevada's tongue drew a soft moan from Eden. Slowly he took complete possession of her mouth once more, then began to retreat from her. But she didn't want the kiss to end. She needed more of his taste, his caresses, his elemental male passion. Instinctively her teeth closed on his tongue, silently demanding that he stay within her.

When Eden felt the response that ripped through Nevada at the unexpected caress of her teeth, she would have smiled, but his hands had shifted on her body, finding and stroking her breasts, sending burst after burst of pleasure through her. Her teeth released him as her breath came in with a sound of surprise and passion and she shuddered all the way to her core.

Hard, searching, hungry, Nevada's tongue claimed Eden once more, stroking the sultry softness of her mouth with rhythms of penetration and retreat. His hands moved over her breasts, long fingers stroking, kneading, teasing her until her nipples became a velvet hardness. When he plucked softly at them, the bursts of sensation that had been rippling through Eden merged into hot currents of pleasure that turned her bones to honey.

"Nevada, I can't stand up," Eden said raggedly as she clung to his arms, dizzy with the violence of her own response.

"Don't even try. I can hold you, Eden," Nevada said almost roughly, watching her, feeling her knees sag and at the same time feeling his own strength pouring through his body like a river of fire. "I could hold you in one hand. And I will, but not yet. There are other things I want to do first. A hundred of them. A thousand . . . oh, God, Eden, what are you doing to me?"

Eden opened her eyes, saw Nevada watching her, and wondered how she had ever thought his eyes bleak or cold. They were hot, burning, as hungry as his kiss had been.

"Put your arms around my neck," Nevada said, moving Eden's hands even as he spoke. "Hold on to me."

His hands moved once more, stroking her from hips to shoulders and back again, pressing her closer and closer to his body until she felt the urgency of his arousal. Her response was an instinctive, supple movement of her hips that dragged a groan from deep within him. His arms tightened, locking their bodies together while he moved against her once, twice, three times, and each time he promised himself it would be the last.

And each time it was not.

"Open your mouth and kiss me," Nevada said hoarsely, bending down to Eden. "I have to be inside you and that's the only way. *Kiss me.*"

Eden gave Nevada what he wanted, needing the urgent joining as much as he did. When the world shifted and spun beneath her feet she simply clung more tightly to him, her arms fierce around his neck. He held her close and hard even after he lowered her to his camp mattress and deepened the hungry melding of mouths. He wanted her with a force that he no longer questioned, for thought was impossible. It was all he could do to control himself.

After a long time Nevada shuddered and slowly, reluctantly, ended the kiss. He lifted his head and let breath hiss out between his teeth. Nothing had ever tempted him the way Eden did at that instant, lying warm and undefended in his arms, wanting him until she trembled with it.

"I should have taken that bath in ice water," Nevada said, his eyes closed and his voice rough with his own arousal. When his eyes opened he looked from Eden's mouth to the pulse beating in her throat and the taut nipples pressing up against the green cotton of her blouse. "But it wouldn't have done any good."

"It wouldn't?" Eden asked huskily. "I thought a cold bath always worked."

Nevada shook his head as he bent down to her breasts. "When you throw a bucket of water on a wildfire, all you get is steam."

His teeth closed delicately around one of her nipples, drawing a ragged gasp of surprise from Eden as pleasure streaked through her body, arching her against Nevada in sensual reflex.

"Wildfire," Nevada said thickly, arching into Eden in return. "Clean and beautiful and hotter than hell. Are you going to let me undress you or do you want to play it safe?"

"I'm always safe with you, Nevada. No matter what. I knew that the first time I saw you."

Thick, black lashes swept down, concealing the smoldering green of Nevada's eyes. Eden's hands stroked his hair, his beard, his mustache, and she smiled as she gently kissed him.

"Undress me, Nevada," she whispered, touching the tip of her tongue to his lips. "I've wanted to feel your beard on my skin for so long. I have to... feel you."

His hands moved from Eden's throat to her waist. Cloth fell away, revealing the creamy feminine curves of her breasts. Being bared to the waist was new to her. She blushed until she saw the look in Nevada's eyes. The passion and appreciation in his glance made her forget that she had never given herself in this way before.

The necklace with its tiny ring of braided gold gleamed softly against Eden's throat. Nevada bent and brushed the small ring with his lips, then pierced the golden circle with the tip of his tongue, touching the warm skin beneath. The intimacy of the instant made pain and pleasure twist deeply inside him, foretaste of what would happen if he let control slip from him.

Nevada knew he should stop now, leaving Eden as untouched as he had found her; and he knew he would not, could not walk away. Not yet. She was too beautiful, too warm, and he had been too long without warmth and beauty.

His hands moved, skimming the curves and peaks of Eden's bare breasts. She gasped as something deep within her shimmered and burst into fire. With a combination of hunger and anticipation, Nevada watched her rosy nipples tighten beneath his touch until they pouted and begged for his mouth. But he had seen Eden's first blush, sensed the instant of uncertainty when her breasts were bared to his eyes, his hands.

"I could hold you down and devour you," Nevada said huskily, aching to taste all the shades of pink and cream, to know all the feminine textures of Eden's body. "And you know it, don't you?

Would you mind my mouth on you? Talk to me, Eden. I don't want to shock you or frighten you."

Eden tried to speak just as Nevada's fingertips delicately squeezed one pink crown. A shivering, hot sensation raced through her. She pressed his hands more closely to her breasts and looked into his eyes.

"I'm not frightened, Nevada. I know that you'll never use your strength against me, and that's all that matters."

Eden lifted one hand and ran her fingertips over Nevada's beard, over his mustache, over his lips, then dipped into the sultry heat of his mouth in a sensuous foray that made his breath break. She laughed softly at his surprise.

"As for shocking me," Eden whispered, "some of the thoughts I'm having right now just might shock *you*. I'm inexperienced, not frightened or repelled. Touch me however you want to. Teach me how you want to be touched. Because I want to touch you, Nevada. I want to give you what you want, what you need, everything you ever dreamed. I want . . . everything."

For long moments Nevada fought a pitched battle for self-control. Eden couldn't know what she was doing to him, what she was offering him, what he wanted so fiercely since he had seen her walking toward him in West Fork and heard summer call to him in a husky voice.

Eden was a gift he shouldn't take.

She was a gift he couldn't refuse.

"Eden . . ."

Nevada tried to say more. No words came that equaled his need. What did come was a silent vow that he would unwrap her gift gently, using the discipline learned in war to bring pleasure rather than pain to the woman who was watching him with all the colors of life in her eyes, all the passions of living in her voice, every emotion he had vowed never to feel whispering to him, promising him . . . everything.

Heaven and hell and the rainbow burning between.

Nevada curled his tongue around Eden's caressing finger, sucked, bit gently, and released her.

"Does that mean you won't mind if I take off your shoes and socks?" he asked softly.

Eden smiled.

With a swift motion Nevada shifted until he was kneeling at her feet. Before Eden could take a deep breath he had slipped off her shoes and slid his index fingers beneath the top of her socks, circling her ankles, stroking her, making her gasp at the unexpected sensitivity of her own skin. With a smooth movement he stripped her socks away, leaving her feet naked. He fitted a palm against the arch of each foot, rubbed slowly, and watched unexpected pleasure transform Eden's expression.

"You know my body better than I do," she said. "Your hands are so warm and hard. I love your hands, Nevada."

He turned and rubbed his beard against her instep, heard her breath break, felt her shiver. His teeth closed gently while the tip of his tongue drew a line of fire beneath her arch. Her toes curled and she made a breathless sound. Slowly he released her feet. His hands stroked from her ankles up the length of her legs and then on to the waistband of her jeans. There he stopped and looked into her eyes.

"Whatever you want," Eden said, huskily. "Just tell me what to do, Nevada. Tell me how to please you, too."

"Your trust..." Nevada's eyes closed, then opened brilliant with an emotion that was as great as his passion and as deep as his pain. "Fairy-tale girl, having you give yourself to me is more pleasure than I've ever known."

Nevada bent and brushed his mouth over Eden's lips, the tiny ring lying in the hollow of her throat, the taut velvet tips of her breasts. Soft sounds came from her, sighs like flames rippling higher as her jeans were smoothed caressingly down her body by Nevada's hard and gentle hands. When Eden realized that she was naked and he was looking at her, she trembled. He fitted his palm over her pale, soft triangle of curls and eased his long fingers between her legs, holding her in one hand, covering her vulnerable softness completely.

"It's all right," Nevada whispered against Eden's mouth. "You're not naked anymore."

His hand moved gently, rocking against flesh that was already humid, sensitized. Her breath broke, caught, broke again as something shimmered and burst softly, repeatedly, inside her, melting her against his hand. He felt the unmistakable heat of her response and groaned even as he searched through the hot curls.

"Kiss me, Eden. Let me inside you."

Eden parted her lips and felt the hot, gliding penetration of Nevada's tongue and his finger at the same time. The startled sound she made was transformed into a throaty cry of passion that he drank as he deepened the twin caresses, exploring and pleasuring her with the same slow movements. The repeated sensual forays sent more shimmering waves expanding through her, melting her around him.

All thought of shyness fled Eden, leaving her in the grip of enthralling passion. When Nevada's touch redoubled, filling her, Eden shivered and cried out. He drank that cry, too, and his caresses deepened as his thumb slid over the sleek hard nub of desire he had called from her softness.

Sensual lightning searched through every cell in Eden's body, drawing a surprised cry from her.

Deliberately Nevada closed his teeth on her neck, both distracting her and paradoxically increasing the intensity of her body's response to the hot, intimate movements of his hand. His thumb returned again and again, spreading the liquid fire of her response, teasing her, inciting her, urging her higher and higher, drawing the sensual tension in her tighter and tighter until finally her breath stopped and pleasure burst, drenching her with sweet fire.

Gently Nevada withdrew his touch. He gathered Eden against himself and held her, trying to ignore the violence of his own unsatisfied need. It was impossible. Every breath he took was spiced with her fragrance, infused with her warmth, and the soft weight of her body against his made him burn.

After several minutes Eden sighed, stirred, and said softly, "You were right. My hands aren't shaking anymore." She kissed the base of Nevada's neck and felt the instant speeding of his pulse and the shiver that went through his body. "But yours still are."

"I'll live," he said tightly.

"I'm glad to hear that, because I'm going to need your help." She slid from Nevada's arms and went to work on the laces of his walking boots.

"Eden, what are you doing?"

"Taking off your boots."

"I can see that," he said roughly.

She smiled. "I thought you could." She pulled off one boot and sock, then the other. "Watch closely and you can see me taking off your jeans, too."

Nevada's hands flashed out, grabbing Eden's wrists as she reached for his waistband. Smoldering green eyes searched her face.

"You don't have to," he said.

"Would it shock you to know that I want to? You have a beautiful body, Nevada. Touching you would be like stroking a big cat, all steely muscle and satin pelt."

Nevada's eyes closed as he bit back a groan of need. The realization of how close he was to the limits of his self-control shocked him.

"Not now, Eden," he said roughly.

She leaned forward, bracing herself against Nevada's hard torso. Her mouth sought his. When his lips refused to open, she ran the tip of her tongue across them.

"Yes, now," she breathed.

"You ask too much of me," Nevada said in a low, savage voice. "What happens if half a loaf isn't enough for me? What if I lose control and take you? I could get you pregnant!"

As Eden looked down the length of Nevada's body, her eyes changed, becoming a luminous golden green. "Yes, you certainly could."

The approval in Eden's voice was as seductive as the glide of her tongue over his lips had been. Nevada closed his eyes, no longer able to bear the sight of Eden kneeling naked by his side. He wanted her hands all over his skin, he wanted her mouth, he wanted her hot, silky body fitted to him.

Nevada didn't know he had released Eden's hands until he heard the first metal snap on his shirt open. The other snaps followed in slow succession, for Eden was enjoying each new bit of masculine territory that was revealed by the steady retreat of his black flannel shirt. Finally she tugged the shirt-tails free of his jeans and ran her hands almost greedily over his chest.

The pleasure Eden took in touching Nevada made the air wedge in his throat. She was smiling dreamily while her fingers kneaded through the wedge of black hair that began at his collarbone and narrowed to a finger's width just above his navel. When she smoothed her way back to Nevada's chest and bent to kiss him, her breasts swayed against him with soft invitation. She shivered as the cushion of hair on his chest teased her nipples to life once more.

"I'm new to this," Eden whispered, moving again, this time deliberately, increasing the sweet friction of her breasts against Nevada's chest. "But I'm assuming that men and women like the same kind of touching." Her hands searched through the rough silk of his chest hair, seeking and finding the flat male nipples, teasing them into hard points. "If I'm wrong, let me know."

Nevada's breath hissed between his teeth as pleasure lanced through his body, tightening it as surely as the male nipples hardening beneath Eden's fingertips. This time when her tongue traced his lips, they opened hungrily, both accepting and demanding a deep mating of mouths. By the time the kiss ended, his skin was slick with a sultry sheen of passion and he was breathing much too hard.

Knowing he shouldn't, needing Eden too much to stop himself, Nevada lifted her astride his half-naked body and took the pink tip of one breast into his mouth. As he shaped her with the changing pressures of teeth and tongue, he felt the sudden arching of her back, the clenching of her thighs, and the secret rain of her passion. He groaned and pulled her more deeply into his mouth, loving her responsive flesh.

"I'm supposed to be—pleasuring you—not the other way around," Eden said, fighting for the breath that had deserted her without warning.

After a last, lingering love bite, Nevada released her breast and whispered, "Turning you on pleasures me."

Before Eden could answer, Nevada's mouth moved to her other breast. He licked its pink peak until Eden shivered and her nipple tightened in a rush that made her moan. His lips parted hungrily as he took all of her sweet flesh that he would into the heat and darkness of his mouth.

"It's dangerous, though," Nevada said finally, his voice thick.

He released Eden with a slow reluctance that was itself a caress. She trembled again, and again Nevada felt her hot, secret rain against his naked skin. He swore softly, shockingly, even as one hand traced her spine to the small of her back and from there down the warm cleft below until she gasped in pleasure once more.

"Too damned dangerous," he whispered.

"W-why?"

One of Nevada's hands flattened between Eden's shoulder blades, pressing her tightly against his chest, while his other hand explored the warmth that now lay open to his touch. Eden's breath went out in a moan as Nevada caressed the swollen, sultry flesh that had known only his touch. His fingertips glided inside, drawing forth more of Eden's secret rain.

Nevada's hand retreated, returned, caressed, and when Eden moaned, so did he. His hand retreated and there was a muted sound of metal buttons opening one at a time. Gently, inexorably, Nevada's hands eased Eden's weight farther down his body until the hard length of his arousal pressed up between her legs. Only the thickness of his underwear prevented the joining of their bodies.

The barrier was not nearly enough for safety.

"That's why it's dangerous," Nevada said savagely.

For a moment Eden couldn't answer. The elemental fitting of male against female had just taught her how much had been missing from her previous taste of passion. The realization was dizzying, like the heat spreading up in waves from between her thighs, wildfire melting her. Instinctively she moved her hips, rocking slowly, softly, hotly, getting as close as she could to the hard male flesh despite the barrier of cloth.

Nevada had meant to shock Eden from her passion with the blunt reminder of his arousal, but he was the one who was shocked. The melting response of Eden's body spread through the thin barrier between them as though nothing were there at all.

And then nothing was.

A sweep of his hands, a muscular twist of his body and Nevada lay naked between Eden's legs. She made a soft sound of discovery and approval at the new masculine territory he had given to her. He watched through narrowed green eyes while her fingertips caressed and traced hot satin skin, learning the contours of his hunger, capturing the single drop of passion he could not contain.

Eden lifted a fingertip to her lips, touched it to her tongue. "Now I know what life tastes like."

A groan was dragged out of the depths of Nevada's soul. His hands moved, lifting, seeking, finding, joining his body with Eden. He tried not to join with her completely. Then he saw that she was watching him take her and her eyes were like sunrise, burning away darkness, hungry for the day to come. Her name was torn from him and he pierced the veil of her innocence in a single incandescent instant.

Eden's breath unraveled as she accepted the transformation, taking all of Nevada until she was hot and sleek around him, fully alive and lush with the secret rain of her passion, and his name was a chant on her lips. As she bent to kiss him, the motion shifted her body around him, caressing him with silky urgency, calling to him in a communication far older and more potent than words.

"Don't move," Nevada said hoarsely.

"Why?" Eden breathed, moving, shivering, moving again, because she had never felt anything so perfect as being joined with the man she loved.

"I can't—control—"

Even as Nevada's voice broke he reached for Eden, drawing her mouth down to his, hungry for every bit of her. He rolled over swiftly, taking her with him, pinning her with his hips, making it impossible for her to move. Shaking with the violence of his restraint, Nevada began to withdraw from Eden.

But when only a last, tantalizing fraction joined them, Nevada found he couldn't force himself to leave Eden completely. Body rigid, he fought for the self-control that had been his only weapon and defense against life's treachery.

Eden's voice broke over Nevada's name. She shivered and whispered fragments of words, passionate sounds without meaning, pleading and demanding, knowing only that she must be completely joined with him again or die.

"Once more, fairy-tale girl," Nevada breathed against Eden's lips. "Just once."

Slowly he pressed into Eden again, filling her, feeling her cling to him with tiny, hot movements that were as involuntary as the wild beating of her heart. He withdrew even more slowly, and once again could not force himself to leave her entirely. Fists clenched, eyes tightly shut, skin gleaming with sweat, Nevada fought to make his body obey the demands of his mind.

Then Eden moaned and the wild, sensual rain of her release bathed Nevada in fire, burning through all possibility of control. With an anguished sound he thrust into her once more, filling her, giving himself to her with each elemental surge of his body until the gift was finally complete.

And then Nevada lay spent on Eden's breast, felt their hearts beating together, tasted their mingled breaths, and understood the full extent of his self-betrayal.

My God, how could I be such a fool?

The only answer was as bitter as it was true. The self-discipline that had been the very core of Nevada's survival had been breached at the same instant as the frail barrier of Eden's innocence. He could not have been more foolish. She could not have wounded him more savagely if she had slid a knife between his ribs into his heart.

Silently Nevada withdrew from Eden, dressed swiftly and walked away. With each step he prayed he would have the strength to build his defenses once more, and this time build them so high and so deep that he would never again be touched by the devastation of Eden's sweet and fatal fire.

10

As always when Baby was around, Eden woke up at dawn. As had become her habit in the past week, she looked automatically to the place where Nevada's bedroll had been.

It was empty.

It had been empty for seven days. She had no reason to believe it wouldn't always be empty. Nevada had made love to her, made her cry out with the pleasure and beauty of his touch—and then he had left without a word. He hadn't been back since.

Silently Eden asked the question that had been aching inside her every moment since she had awakened alone.

Why did you leave, Nevada? When I asked you why you hated wanting me, you told me it was because you didn't have me. Then we made love and you walked away as though nothing had happened. Why, Nevada? Didn't I please you?

Blinking back the tears that would do no good, Eden got up and quickly began preparing her breakfast. Her breath made silver-white plumes in the cabin's cold air. The chinook had been followed by a cold northern wind that had settled in as though it meant to stay until June. Last night a thin veil of snow had fallen once more over the land, making the ground glitter whitely.

"If that mama cougar has gone hunting, we'll find her tracks. Then I'll finally find her den. Right, Baby?" Eden asked, her voice husky from lack of use.

The big animal's ears pricked alertly at her first word. His yellow eyes had a gemlike clarity as they followed Eden's every motion until breakfast was eaten and the cabin was put in order.

"Ready to go tracking?"

Instantly Baby was on his feet, vibrating with eagerness. He pawed at the front door.

"I thought you would be. This time let's find something bigger than a bobcat."

Baby whined and pranced, understanding only that his favorite activity was about to begin.

Vowing to think only about cougars rather than the man who had touched her soul and then walked away as though nothing had happened, Eden opened the door and let Baby out. He shot across the clearing and raced into the sparse forest like a low-flying shadow.

Eden slipped on her backpack and walked quickly out into the light. The tracks Baby left were crisp, clear, and unnecessary. She knew where he was going—to the creek in the bottom of a ravine, and up the opposite slope to the base of the big fir tree where the cougar had first been spotted. The cat had managed to elude her trackers since the wild chase two weeks ago.

While looking for the mama cougar, Eden had found the tracks of two other cougars, photographed them, logged them, and followed them as far as possible. One of the cougars had been a young cat searching for territory that was unoccupied by other cougars. The boundary markers left by resident cougars had discouraged the young cat, pushing it along until it was beyond the boundaries of Eden's study area.

The second cougar whose tracks Eden had found was apparently a permanent resident, but it didn't have a den, which meant that it wasn't a female with cubs. Cougars without cubs covered as much as thirty miles in a day. Following such animals was very difficult, even when Baby's nose was thrown into the effort. In bad weather, tracking cats without radio collars was impossible.

Eden had pinned her hopes on Nevada's belief that the "big tree cougar" was a mama. The fact that the cat had vanished for the past two weeks was encouraging rather than discouraging. It probably meant that the fir tree was more toward the edge of the cougar's territory than in its center, and the cubs were keeping her close to home. But a mama cougar nursing cubs had to eat to keep up her own strength, which meant she had to go out and hunt. Hunting cats left tracks, especially in freshly fallen snow.

When Eden reached the big tree, Baby was casting about for fresh scent. When he found none, he looked to Eden. She whistled. Baby shot off along the shoulder of the rise, quartering a new area. She followed his progress, whistling or calling occasional instructions, communicating with him in a code that the two of them had worked out over years of hunting together.

Three hours later and seven miles distant from the big tree, Baby struck fresh tracks. His howl electrified the silent land. Instantly Eden whistled for Baby to return to her. He obeyed on the run, mouth wide, pink tongue lolling, laughing up at her when he found her.

At Eden's signal, Baby fell in step at her left heel. So long as Baby hadn't been penned up for days, he was more than happy to collaborate on the hunt. In the past week, he had gotten plenty of exercise. Eden had spent as little time as possible within the cabin, for it was haunted by Nevada's absence.

A few minutes later Eden was studying the tracks Baby had found. They were indeed fresh. More important, they had been left by the cougar Baby had once treed. The slightly oversize toe on the cat's left front paw was unmistakable. Eagerly Eden followed the tracks, moving quickly. The forest thinned even more, giving way to a boulder-strewn, south-facing slope. The tracks suddenly became very close together, almost overlapping. Abruptly the tracks dug in hard and deep—and vanished.

Eden paced off the length of empty snow until the tracks began again and whistled soft approval.

"Thirty-three feet in a single bound. Not bad for a young female."

Through binoculars, Eden scanned the landscape immediately in front of her. The wind gusted, shifting and swirling down the slope, blowing from her back rather than across her face.

Suddenly Baby threw back his head and howled.

"Quiet," Eden said without putting down the glasses.

Baby yapped and danced.

"Heel."

Baby heeled. And whined very softly.

"Settle down, Baby," Eden said impatiently, still scanning the landscape. "What's gotten into you?"

"Me."

The sound of Nevada's deep voice made Eden spin around and stare in disbelief. The first thing she noticed was that Nevada had a rifle slung across his back. The second thing she noticed was his eyes. They were as cold as the wind, as dispassionate as the sky, and full of shadows so bleak they made Eden want to cry out in pain.

"There was a decent tracking snow," Nevada said, "so Luke sent me back up here to help you."

Like his eyes, his voice lacked emotion.

"Sent you," Eden repeated. "I see."

She turned back and began scanning the landscape with a composure that was pure desperation. Her heart was beating much too hard, too fast, and her hands would have shaken if she hadn't gripped the binoculars until her knuckles showed white.

Luke sent me. Sent me. Sent me.

The words echoed in Eden's mind, slicing into her. Nevada couldn't have made it clearer that he hadn't sought her out for any reason other than a direct order from the owner of the Rocking M.

"Tell Luke thank-you, but it's not necessary," Eden said when she could trust her voice once more. "Baby and I do our best work alone."

"Luke didn't ask if you needed me. He told me to check on you."

"You have. I'm fine."

Narrowly Nevada surveyed the straight line of Eden's back. He heard her words, but he couldn't accept them. Her voice belonged to a stranger, flat where Eden's had been vibrant, thin where hers had been rich.

"You don't sound fine," he said.

She said nothing more.

Nevada swore beneath his breath. He walked silently up to Eden, not wanting to get any closer to her but unable to stop himself. As he moved, his body was tight with the conflict that had been tearing him apart since his self-control had broken and he had taken and surrendered to Eden in the same passionate instant.

"Damn it, I didn't want it to be this way," Nevada said harshly. "I didn't want you to be hurt."

Eden lowered the glasses. They were useless anyway, for she was crying too hard to see anything but her own tears.

"Is that why you left without so much as a word to me?" she asked. "To keep from hurting me?"

"What was I supposed to do, tell you fairy tales about love? I won't lie to you, fairy-tale girl. You knew it when you came to me at the cabin and burned me alive."

Abruptly Nevada stopped speaking. Memories of Eden's incandescent sensuality were lightning strokes of pain that scored him repeatedly, giving him no peace, ripping through new defenses and old, scoring across the unhealed past, threatening to touch him as he had vowed never to be touched again.

And he fought his hunger as he had never fought anything except death itself. Wanting, not wanting, fighting himself and her, trapped in an agonizing vise, Nevada turned Eden to face him and saw the silver glitter of her tears.

"Don't you understand?" Nevada whispered savagely. *"I can't be what you want me to be."*

She closed her eyes. "A man who believes in love."

"Yes," he said flatly. His hard thumbs tilted up her face to his and his fingers trembled against her skin. "I told Luke I wouldn't come up here. He told me I could take his orders or I could pack up and leave the Rocking M. I packed, but I couldn't let you run me off the only home I have, so I came up here knowing I would hurt you all over again."

"Nevada," Eden whispered, reaching to him.

"No! I don't want to hurt you again, but it will happen just the same unless you stop asking me to kiss you every time you look at my mouth, stop asking me to touch you every time you look at my hands, stop asking..." Nevada's eyes closed, then opened once more, clear and hard and cold. "I would sell my soul not to want you, Eden, but the devil took my soul a long time ago and I want you like hell burning."

As Eden looked at Nevada's silver-green eyes, a chill moved over her. He was a wild animal caught in a trap...and she was that trap. The knowledge was in his eyes, shadows and bleakness, watchfulness and calculation and fear, and most of all in his pain, an agony that drew Nevada's mouth into a hard line.

His pain was as real as the unsheathed claws of his honesty.

Eden took a deep, shaking breath and acknowledged the truth. "I understand. You won't love me. I can't help loving you. Too bad, how sad, and all of that. Meanwhile, the earth turns and the seasons change and babies are born and some die and there's not a damn thing we can do about that, either."

"Eden . . ."

She waited, hoping in spite of herself.

"Eden, I . . ." Nevada made an odd, almost helpless gesture with his hand.

After a few more moments Eden smiled with the bittersweet acceptance that she had learned after Aurora's death.

"It's all right, Nevada. I was warned going in, and several other times along the way, and that's more than we usually get out of life. You don't have to love me. I'm yours without it, if you want me. And even if you don't."

Nevada's jaw tightened against the pain of Eden's acceptance of what he was and was not. "That's not . . ." he began, then his throat constricted again, taking away his ability to speak.

"Fair?" she suggested.

Eden's smile was as sad and enigmatic as her changing hazel eyes. Nevada looked away, unable to bear what he was doing to her.

"I thought you didn't believe in fairy tales, warrior."

"I don't."

"Then don't talk to me about 'fair.' If life were fair, my sister would have celebrated her sixth birthday today. But life isn't and she didn't and wailing about it won't change one damned thing."

Nevada looked back slowly. His eyes were intent, fierce. "You really mean that."

"I always say what I mean. It's a failing of mine."

"You don't believe in fairy tales, but you do believe in love," he said, unable to understand. "Knowing what life truly is, you still allow yourself to love." He hesitated, not wanting to hurt Eden any more but unable to stop himself from asking, "How can you?"

Eden looked into the untamed depths of Nevada's eyes and saw a curiosity that was as great as his wariness, as intense as his passion...a wolf circling closer and closer to the beckoning campfire, pulled toward the flames against his deepest instinct of self-preservation, enthralled by the radiant possibilities of fire.

"How can I do anything else?" Eden said simply. "Man is the animal that wrote Ecclesiastes and still laughed, still loved, still lived. Not just survival, Nevada. *Living.*"

Silence stretched, stretched, then was broken by a harsh word. Nevada pointed off to the right, where a deer had left tracks along the margin of the open forest.

"Follow those tracks, Eden. They'll tell you all you need to know about the true nature of *living.*"

Without a word Eden signaled for Baby to heel and began following the deer tracks, knowing what she would find. The mama cougar was alive, which meant that other life must die to sustain the cat's own life. It had always been that way. It always would be. Life fed. It was the very thing that distinguished life from death.

The deer tracks ended in a turmoil of snow and muddy earth. Cougar tracks led away. The cat had been walking easily despite the limp burden of the deer clenched in its jaws and the hooved feet dragging across the snow.

"A quick, clean kill," Eden said calmly, reading the tracks. "There's nothing surprising in that. Cougars are among the most efficient predators on earth. All you have to do is watch them move and you know that they're supremely adapted for the hunt and the kill."

She waited, but Nevada said nothing. Taking a deep breath, she turned and confronted the warrior she loved.

"In moose country," she continued, "a cougar will routinely stalk and kill moose that weigh five or even eight times as much as the cat does. Sometimes the moose wins and the cougar is injured. Cats are very tough. It takes them a long time and a horrifying amount of pain before they finally die. When it comes to death, nature is much more cruel to predators than predators are to their own prey."

Nevada simply watched Eden with bleak eyes, saying nothing.

"And man is the only predator who can see into the future," Eden continued in a soft, relentless voice. "Man knows that he, too, will die. That's the crucial difference between us and cougars. Yet, even knowing that we'll die, mankind is capable of creating as well as destroying, of loving as well as hating, of true living as well as sheer animal survival. Violent death is only a part of human reality, and not even the most important part at that."

"And I suppose that love is?" he asked sardonically.

"Yes." Without realizing it, Eden raised her hand to the open collar of her jacket. She touched her throat, reassured by the familiar presence of Aurora's ring. "Love is never wasted," Eden whispered. "Never. But it can hurt like nothing else on earth."

Nevada watched Eden with narrowed eyes, wanting to argue with her, to shake her from her foolish belief in love; yet the words died unspoken, for Eden's pain was very real and not foolish at all.

Saying nothing more, Eden turned away from Nevada, lifted the binoculars, and searched the landscape until she found the place where the cougar had dragged the deer. She examined the remains of the cougar's meal with the eyes of a wildlife biologist rather than those of a woman who loved deer as well as cougars. Usually cats ate their fill, raked debris over the remains and walked off to nap nearby, returning to feed until the carcass was consumed or the remains disturbed by other predators. A careful survey with the glasses allowed Eden to pick up the cougar's tracks without coming close enough to alert the wary animal when it returned to feed.

"Baby. Heel."

The big wolf came to Eden's side instantly, eyes alert, his whole being intent upon the woman who had rescued him from an agonizing steel trap despite his own best attempts to savage the very hands that were helping him. Gently, firmly, Eden's fingers wrapped around Baby's muzzle in a command for silence.

The change that went over the wolf was inde-
scribable. It was as though he had been standing in
shadow and then stepped out into the sun. Past experience told Baby that the command to be quiet
meant that the object of the hunt was probably
close by, and the wolf was a predator from the tip
of his erect ears down to the black pads of his feet.
Walking as though on springs, Baby followed Eden
in a wide semicircle around the deer carcass. When
he came across the fresh cat tracks, he bristled but
made not one sound.

For a mile they followed the tracks. Nevada followed Eden as silently as the wolf did. The cougar's tracks led up a long, shallow rise where trees
offered only sparse cover, if any at all. Where the
snow had melted through, a distinct green blush
covered the ground. Despite the intermittent snow
squalls, spring wasn't going to be denied.

Partway up the slope it became obvious that if
the cougar—or the cougar's den—was on the far
side, Nevada and Eden would be spotted as soon as
their heads cleared the rise. Eden didn't want to
panic the cat, perhaps sending it on a search for a
new den for its cubs. All she wanted to do was find
the cougar's tracks and follow them to the den,
where she could watch the cat from a distance so as
not to disturb the animal.

Frowning, Eden tested wind direction with a wet
fingertip. She tested again and shrugged. The wind

was weak, but unpredictable. Thankfully, scent wasn't nearly the problem it would have been if she had been tracking wolves. Cougars depended on their eyes and ears rather than their noses.

Eden stopped, looked at the gentle slope rising ahead of her, and sighed. It would be a cold, wet and sometimes muddy crawl, but there was no help for it if she hoped to get to the top without giving away her presence. She slipped out of her back-pack, but before she set it aside, Nevada went past her like a black wraith. He had removed his hat and backpack but had kept his rifle.

Crouching, taking advantage of every scrap of cover, crawling on hands and knees and finally on his stomach, Nevada went up the slope with a speed and silence that sent a shiver over Eden. He moved like a cougar—confident, soundless, graceful, and potentially deadly.

Let me tell you what the real world is like, fairy-tale girl... you walk through a narrow mountain pass in single file with five handpicked men and arrive at your destination and look around and you're alone, nothing on the back trail but blood and silence.

Nevada eased up behind the cover of a bush, slowly pulled his binoculars out of his jacket, and began quartering the slope below. The cougar's tracks continued, zigzagging across a boulder field where ancient trees had fallen like jackstraws. The tracks vanished. They didn't reappear anywhere on the new snow beyond.

Patiently Nevada scanned the boulders, looking for several big stones canted together to create a sheltered hollow, or for an uprooted tree, or for any irregularity in the land that would provide a den for a mama cougar and her cubs. Finally he spotted a collection of boulders with an opening at their base where a tree had blown down and created a small cave between the uprooted tree and the rocks. In the darkness of the hollow lay a long, tawny shadow.

Nevada focused the glasses and found himself looking at the white muzzle, wheat-colored cheeks and sleek black facial markings of an adult female cougar. There was no doubt about the cat's sex, for she was lying on her side while three spotted cubs nursed enthusiastically.

Slowly Nevada put down the glasses and looked until he spotted the den once more. He memorized landmarks, cover, approaches, and the general lie of the land with the thoroughness of a man whose life had depended on knowing just such information in the past. When he was satisfied that he could find the den again, he retreated down the slope as swiftly and silently as he had gone up it.

Eden waited for him at the bottom, a silent question in her eyes. He nodded and slid his hand up along her cheek, holding her while he bent down until he could speak directly against her ear. Although there was little chance of the cat's hearing them, Nevada knew that voices carried an astonishing distance in the snowy silence.

"She's denned up about two hundred feet beyond the far side of the rise," he said softly. "She has three cubs."

A shiver coursed through Eden's body, but it came from the touch of Nevada's hand rather than from the news about the mama cougar.

"Did she sense you?" Eden asked, her voice low and soft.

"No." Nevada lowered his hand. "She's still sleeping off her meal. I doubt that she'll be out and about before sunset. Maybe not even then."

"Do you have a clear field of view from the ridge?"

"Pretty good. It would be even better from there," he said, pointing to a spot farther along the crest, "but that's the way she went from her kill to the den. I didn't figure you wanted to leave tracks there."

"Not until she's finished with the deer," Eden agreed.

Eden tried to think about possible hiding places, places to build a blind for observation, places where the cougar wouldn't be likely to find them and become alarmed; but all she could think about at that instant was how close Nevada was, and how much closer he had been seven days ago.

Motionless, Nevada watched Eden's changing hazel eyes and the delicate pressure of her teeth against her lower lip and the fiddling of her fingers over his jacket hem while she thought about other things. If she had been aware of her actions, Nevada would have been angry. But he knew she wasn't aware of what she was doing. Unfortunately, that knowledge did nothing to counter the sudden hard rush of his blood when her hand brushed against his jeans. He captured her fingers and placed them on his beard.

"If you have to pet me while you think, keep it above the waist."

Eden flushed. "I didn't mean—"

"I know," Nevada interrupted tightly. "You weren't thinking about what you were doing. But I was. I like being petted by you. I like it way too much. The ground is cold and hard and wet, but I wouldn't care, and after a few minutes you wouldn't, either. The mama cougar might get kind of curious, though. You make such wild sounds when I'm buried in you."

Eden's color deepened to scarlet.

"Don't," Nevada said in a husky voice, knowing he shouldn't speak but unable to help himself. "I like hearing you, feeling you, smelling you, tasting you. I liked it too damn much. You were a virgin, but you took all of me and shivered with pleasure..." He let breath rush out between his teeth in a hissing curse. "I came up here for cougars, not sex. So get on up that slope and watch your mama cat, fairy-tale girl. I'll circle around and reconnoiter the far side."

Nevada turned and walked off, heading away from the rise, moving with the easy, powerful stride that was as much a part of him as his pale green eyes. Eden watched him for a full minute before she took a ragged breath, turned around and went up the rise, following the tracks Nevada had made.

I came up here for cougars, not sex.

The words hurt, but he had no more meant to hurt her than she had meant for her absentminded fidgeting to arouse him.

You wouldn't have gotten sex from me, Nevada Blackthorn. You never have. You never will. What I gave you was love, not sex, and somewhere deep inside your stubborn warrior soul you know it.

Don't you?

There was no answer but the one implicit in the nickname Nevada had given to her.

Fairy-tale girl.

11

Swearing under his breath, Nevada lay beneath a sky so black no stars could be seen and listened to the thunder rumbling and churning overhead. He had eaten meals with Eden since he had returned to Wildfire Canyon, but he had slept outside the cabin—much to Baby's delight. Tonight, however, the wolf had shown the innate good sense of a wild animal; at the first cannonade of thunder, Baby had gone to scratch at the cabin door. Curling up to sleep on a few feet of comfortable snow was one thing. Sleeping beneath a barrage of hail mixed with slush was quite another. A wolf had no compunctions about grabbing whatever shelter was available.

Grimly Nevada wished that spring would just settle down and get the job done rather than teetering from snowstorm to chinook and back again, turning sky and ground into a battlefield that was spectacular when viewed from a snug shelter, and a real pain in the butt otherwise.

Quit whining, Nevada told himself as hail hammered down, breaching the uncertain shelter beneath the evergreen where he had dragged his sleeping bag when the storm first had awakened him. *You've been a lot more uncomfortable and survived just fine.*

Yeah, but I wasn't lying thirty feet from Eden, watching her shadow move across curtains while she took her nightly bath, watching her and imagining . . . too damn much.

That was hours ago. She's asleep by now. You should be, too.

Nevada rolled over, scrunched down in the sleeping bag and pulled the waterproof tarp over his head. He tried to ignore the icy fingers of slush that found every possible entrance into his sleeping bag. It was difficult. Each time he thought he had defended every bit of exposed territory, the storm discovered another opening. Sleep was impossible.

So was controlling a mind that was as unruly as the storm. Nevada found himself wondering if Eden had stood outside the cabin after dinner and watched his own shadow on the curtains while he had his turn with soap and washrag. Then he wondered if the storm made Eden nervous. If it did, maybe she would like something more interesting than a wolf to keep her hands busy.

Lightning shattered the night into a billion brilliant shards. Thunder followed like a falling mountain, flattening everything in its path. Overhead, Nevada's meager shelter tossed and moaned while evergreen branches shed hail, slush and ice water over him in endless, unpredictable streams. The tarp turned aside some of the storm, but not nearly enough.

What would you call a commando who slept in ice water when there was a warm, safe shelter nearby? Nevada asked himself tauntingly.

A bloody damned fool.

Then I guess you're a bloody damned fool, aren't you? Or are you afraid Eden will creep up on you and ravish you while you sleep?

More likely she'll cut my throat. Since I told her I didn't come up here for sex, she's done everything but climb trees to avoid touching me.

And you're grateful for that, right?

Yeah, right. I'm grateful as all hell on fire.

Nevada wished he could lie to himself convincingly, but that kind of lying wasn't a survival trait, and if Nevada was good at anything, it was surviving.

Sure you are, mocked the voice inside his head. *That's why you're lying out here slowly turning into a Popsicle. Some survivor. You don't even have enough sense to come in out of the rain.*

Branches bent in a gust of wind that lifted a corner of the tarp just in time to let ice water gush over the back of Nevada's undefended neck. With a savage word he shot to his feet, grabbed the tarp and the damp sleeping bag, and stalked up to the cabin.

The door opened before he could raise his fist to knock.

"There's a towel by the fire," Eden said, turning away from Nevada even as she spoke.

With eyes that reflected the leap of flames he watched her retreat. He knew she was making no effort to be sexy yet the motion of her hips beneath the clinging scarlet of her ski underwear was so feminine that it loosened his knees.

Lightning bleached the interior of the cabin in the instant before Nevada closed the door. Baby lay sleeping soundly in the coldest part of the cabin. The wolf didn't even lift his head at Nevada's entrance.

"Go back to sleep," Nevada said, watching Eden retreat.

If Eden said anything in response, it was lost in a crash of thunder. Nevada watched from the corner of his eye as she slid gracefully into the soft folds of her bedding. He peeled off his black T-shirt and grabbed the towel. The terry cloth was warm against his chilled skin. The knowledge that Eden had deliberately heated the towel by the fire in case he came in out of the storm made the brush of the cloth even more pleasurable on his skin. The thought of having Eden's sweet, warm hands on his body instead of the towel made blood rush heavily. His hands clenched on the towel as he fought his response to Eden.

Stop thinking about it.

Right. And while I'm at it, I'll stop breathing, too.

Nevada's hands went to the buttons of his cold, damp jeans. He hesitated, remembering that he had nothing on but clammy denim, then shrugged and resumed undressing. He doubted that Eden was watching him. Even if she was, she had seen him dead naked once before and hadn't fainted at the sight.

A memory exploded in Nevada with a force so great it nearly sent him to his knees—Eden warm across his thighs, touching him intimately, cherishing his hunger, tasting him, whispering of life itself.

Savagely Nevada whipped off his damp jeans, wadded them up and fired them across the cabin. The soft thump of cloth against wood couldn't conceal the sound of the sudden rush of air through Eden's lips when she saw his profile outlined by firelight and knew beyond doubt the hunger raging in him.

"Nevada..." Her husky whisper shivered like firelight in the silence.

Slowly Nevada turned toward Eden. Fighting himself every second, losing every second, Nevada began walking over the cold wooden floor, pulled against his will one slow step at a time until at last he stood by the edge of Eden's mattress, breathing deeply, trying to stop the fine trembling of his hands. He could not. As though driven by a whip, he closed his eyes and sank to his knees. His hands became fists on the powerful, clenched muscles of his thighs.

A moment later Nevada sensed movement, heard the small sounds of cloth rubbing over cloth as the bedding shifted, and then felt Eden's breath rush warmly over his fists. Light kisses touched his hands, gentling him even as the caresses seared him to the bone. With a ragged sound of pain and pleasure he unclenched his fingers and reached for Eden.

As she came to her knees before him, he eased his fingers deeply into the fragrant silk of her hair, tipped her face up to his hungry lips and locked their mouths in a searing kiss. It wasn't enough. No matter how wild, how sweet, how deep, he couldn't get close enough to her with just a kiss. He couldn't touch her completely. He couldn't bathe in her fire.

"Eden," Nevada said hoarsely, tightening his hands in her hair. "Eden . . . let me . . ."

"Yes," she whispered, not even waiting to find out what he was asking of her.

A shudder rippled through Nevada. His eyes opened. They smoldered with reflected flames as he looked at Eden kneeling in front of him, watching him, wanting him.

"Lift your arms, fairy-tale girl," Nevada said huskily.

As Eden raised her arms, the graceful motion reminded Nevada of the shadows he had seen on the curtains as she bathed. His hands slid from her hair down to the hem of her soft ski top, and then beneath. Watching her at every instant, he slowly eased the scarlet top up her body until the cloth was at her elbows and her breasts were completely bare. Abandoning the cloth still tangled around her elbows, he stroked her upper arms and shoulders, caressing the sensitive skin of her inner arm.

"When I saw your shadow moving while you bathed," Nevada said, bending down to Eden's breasts, "I was so damned jealous of the washcloth I thought I would go crazy. I wanted to be the one rubbing over you, getting you wet, making your skin shine in the firelight."

The satin heat of Nevada's mouth rubbed warmth and dampness over first one of Eden's breasts, then the other, making her tremble. When she would have cast aside her top and lowered her arms to hold him, he moved swiftly, holding her as she had been with her back elegantly arched and her breasts utterly defenseless against his mouth. His tongue circled one nipple, his teeth gently raked, and she gasped with pleasure. Before she could catch her breath, he was softly, completely devouring her.

The sweet, changing pressures of Nevada's mouth on her breasts sent fire streaming through her blood. Eden shivered and his name broke on her lips. His answer was the renewed tugging of his mouth, the sweet stabbing of his tongue, pleasure gathering and bursting until she cried out and he made a low sound of satisfaction and triumph. For long, shivering minutes he pleasured her, holding her suspended between firelight and his hungry mouth. When he finally lifted his head, her breasts were taut, flushed, full, and they shone in the firelight.

Nevada looked at Eden for a long time, memorizing the picture her breasts made. Then his burning glance moved down her body and he shivered with an eagerness he had never known and could barely control. When he spoke his voice was thick, rasping, as caressing as his hungry mouth had been.

"Stand up, fairy-tale girl."

Eden made a sound that was halfway between a laugh and a protest. "I can't."

With a quick motion Nevada swept off Eden's top, freeing her arms. His warm hands slid down her body and his shoulder muscles bunched as he lifted Eden to her feet.

"Brace your hands on my shoulders," he said.

Eden obeyed. Moments later she felt her long ski underwear sliding down her legs, leaving her naked but for the soft scarlet cloth pooled at her ankles. Nevada's hair gleamed blackly as he lifted her right foot free of the cloth, caressed the high arch lovingly with his fingertips and brushed a kiss over her inner thigh. Slowly he released her foot as he rubbed his beard against the warmth and resilience of her thigh. When he reached for her other foot, his beard smoothed over her flesh once more.

"I love your beard," Eden said with a broken sigh of pleasure.

"I'm glad."

Nevada's voice was like his beard, a soft, silken rasp of sensation that made Eden melt. She shivered again as he lifted her other foot, slid off the last of the cloth, caressed her foot and released it.

"Do you like this, too?" he asked.

Eden felt the brush of his beard against her inner thigh, the hot touch of his tongue, and the sweet heat of his lips. For long moments Nevada's mouth moved over her thighs, sliding higher, shifting her subtly, parting her legs a bit more with each gentle kiss. The sight of his dark head against the creamy smoothness of her own skin sent rippling sensations throughout Eden's body, echoing of the supple dance of firelight.

"Nevada?"

Her husky whisper sent a tremor through Nevada. The kiss he was giving her changed, becoming a claiming that was just short of pain and simultaneously a pleasure so intense that it made her moan. Eden gasped. For an instant he froze, afraid that he had hurt her; then he felt the melting heat of her response. His hand shifted, skimming the burning gold delta at the apex of her thighs, seeking her softness, finding it, sliding into her with a caress that made her gasp.

The sight of Nevada touching her so intimately made passion and embarrassment twist hotly through Eden. She pushed against his shoulders, silently asking to be released. It was like pushing against sun-warmed stone. His fingers skimmed her again, gliding in and withdrawing slowly, dragging a ragged moan of pleasure from her that was both his name and a protest. Slowly his head turned up to her until she could see the blazing silver green of his eyes.

"Did I hurt you?" Nevada asked huskily.

Eden shook her head and started to speak, but seeing his mouth so close to her hungry flesh scattered her thoughts. "Watching you—you were looking at me—watching me while you—" Her voice broke on a sensual shudder that she couldn't control.

"Did it embarrass you?" Nevada asked.

She nodded and whispered, "A little."

"Any other objections?"

She bit her lips and shook her head.

"Did you like it?" he asked softly.

"Yes," Eden said, her voice low. "I liked it so much I—"

Her voice shattered into a moan as Nevada stole once more into the shadowed softness only he had ever touched.

"Then close your eyes, fairy-tale girl," he said, gently biting the soft skin of her belly, "or what you're going to see will make you blush to the soles of your perfect feet."

"I don't understand," she whispered.

"Neither do I," Nevada admitted, brushing his bearded cheek against the hot golden curls that so tempted him. "I've never wanted a woman the way I want you. I want all of you. Everything. Every way there is."

His hand moved again, gliding up between Eden's smooth thighs, silently asking that she open herself to his caresses. The slow advance and retreat of his touch tantalized her, making her hungry for more. Compelled by Nevada's gentle seduction of her senses, she shifted her stance with each of his caresses until she was trembling and breathing brokenly, her eyes heavy lidded, almost closed, and her body was open to whatever caress he wanted to give.

The touch of Nevada's tongue astonished and unraveled Eden in the same wild instant. His name was torn from her lips as her nails dug into the flexed power of his shoulders. His response to the sensuous bite of her fingernails was a low sound of pleasure and hunger and anticipation. His big hands shifted quickly and closed around her hips until he held her in a passionate vise. Unerringly his mouth found the satin nub his caresses had teased from her softness. With a tenderness that was all the more shattering for its restraint, he caught her delicately between his teeth, holding her hotly captive while his caressing tongue stripped away all thought of embarrassment or inhibition.

Eden shuddered heavily and made a ragged sound of surprise and pleasure, holding on to Nevada for balance as her own deserted her. The steamy intimacy of Nevada's mouth was a delicious assault against which she had no defense. Nor did she want any, for she trusted the warrior who held her within his grasp, his elemental male sensuality a lesson and a lure to her own feminine response. A searing spiral of sensation whirled around her, driving her higher and higher with each caress until she twisted like fire within Nevada's grasp.

And like fire, Eden burned.

The wild, broken sounds of her ecstasy shivered through Nevada. He caressed her again and again, hungry to hear more of her pleasure, unwilling to release the softness and passionate response of the woman he had only begun to explore. Reluctantly he lowered Eden to the bedding, but even then he could not release her, not completely. His hand curled possessively around the golden nest of curls as he kissed her navel, her breasts, the pulse beating frantically in her neck.

Eden tried to speak but could not. Nevada's palm was against her violently sensitive flesh, rubbing lightly, pressing, and a long finger was dipping into her as though he were sipping her secrets one by one. His name came from her throat in a husky moan as ecstasy speared through her unexpectedly once more, convulsing her secretly—but she had no secrets from Nevada anymore. He was inside her, sipping at her, touching her delicately, sharing her pleasure, watching her. His caress redoubled, deepened, and so did her response.

"Nevada?" Eden whispered, not understanding why he still withheld himself from the passion he had brought to her.

But Nevada understood. "That was one way, fairy-tale girl. This is another." His voice was low, dark, and he spoke without looking away from the picture made by his hand and the smooth, creamy curves of Eden's body. "I want them all. Every last one. There's no tomorrow, no yesterday. There's only the night and the storm and the fire, you and me and . . . this."

Nevada's hand had moved again, taking the world from beneath her body, sending her spinning. She gasped his name and was rewarded by another hot caress.

"Look at me," Eden said huskily.

"I am. I never knew a woman could be so beautiful."

Nevada bent down and traced her satin nub with the tip of his tongue. The sight of him caressing her so intimately sent shock waves through Eden's mind and body. She felt cherished, threatened, protected, wanton, a woman locked within storm and fire and night, and the essence of all three was the warrior with the haunted silver-green eyes and gentle hands.

"I love you," Eden said raggedly. "I love you so much I can't—"

Ecstasy burst, breaking her voice.

"I don't want love," Nevada said, his voice as dark as the shadows pooled in his eyes. With a swift, powerful movement he lay between her legs, poised at the very entrance to the inviting Eden he had made his own. "All I want is *this*. But I shouldn't take you. Unprotected. Undefended." A harsh shudder went the length of his body as he fought against himself, against her. *"Damn you, Eden, you're tearing me apart."*

"Take me," Eden whispered, reaching for Nevada, touching the hot, hard flesh that she desired, loving all of him. "And I'll take you, all of you, lover and warrior and man, everything you want to give, every way there is, no recriminations and no regrets. That's what love is, Nevada, and I'll love you until I die."

With a tearing sound that was both pain and pleasure, Nevada thrust into Eden's silken warmth, joining with her in a union that was both savage and sublime. When he could go no deeper he held himself completely still but for the shudders that racked him as his untamed hunger sought to escape the restraints of his discipline.

Eden wrapped herself around Nevada and held him, feeling each tremor of need that tugged at his control. Her fingertips probed through his hair and then down the rigid muscles of his back and hips, wanting to touch all of him at once, to surround him with loving warmth.

When Eden's slender fingers discovered the shadow cleft between his lean hips and the tight, shockingly sensitive flesh below, Nevada's whole body jerked. Making soft sounds of discovery and pleasure, Eden explored the changing textures of his need. Groaning, Nevada drove even more deeply into her, all defenses stripped away, held lovingly in the palm of Eden's hand.

With a new understanding she felt the primal, shivering pulses of Nevada's release, heard her name breaking again and again on his lips, and whispered her own love against his open mouth. After the last tremors finally faded, Eden felt Nevada's body shift. Remembering the time when he had made love to her and then walked away without a word, she tightened her arms around him.

"Don't leave me," she whispered. "Not yet."

"I won't." Nevada made a harsh sound. "I can't."

She looked into his eyes and saw the savage leap of reflected fire. Before she could speak, he was talking again, his voice raw.

"You asked for all of me. I hope you meant it, fairy-tale girl, because you're going to get what you asked for. Every damn bit of it, everything I have to give."

Nevada's lean hips moved and Eden's breath rushed in at the sensations streaking up from their joined bodies.

"I just had you," Nevada said harshly, his voice as savage as his eyes, "and I'm ready for you again. That's why I walked out on you before. I knew I would take you again and again until finally I didn't even have the strength to lick my lips—*and then I would still want you.* It's never been like that for me with a woman. You're in my blood like fever and my body is on fire. I'm going to do the same thing to you that you're doing to me, fairy-tale girl. I'm going to burn you alive.''

Nevada bent and took Eden's mouth, opening it with a quick twist of his head, searching her softness even as he pinned her beneath the hard weight of his body. One powerful arm slipped beneath her hips, pulling her even closer, holding her so tightly that he could feel her bones beneath her soft flesh and she could feel his. Then he began moving, driving into her, taking all of her again and again, hot skin sliding against hot skin until the sweet friction ignited her soft flesh with an intensity that shocked her.

She called his name wildly and saw his eyes blaze with response. He rocked hard against her and then harder still, fanning the passionate fire, driving into her until sweat gleamed on both their bodies and she cried out as ecstasy raked her with incandescent claws.

And still there was no end, no peace, no safety, for he was still moving inside her in a rhythm as relentless as it was savage, driving her higher and yet higher until Eden felt as though she were going to die, as though she had been ripped from one world and thrust into another and in this one she was on fire. With a wrenching moan she arched into Nevada, burning fiercely, needing even more of him, telling him what she needed with words that also burned.

"You're feeling it now, aren't you?" Nevada said darkly as his teeth scored Eden's ear. "This is what you did to me the first time I saw you, before I ever even touched you, a burning all the way to the marrow of my bones. And then I had you and still it wasn't enough, it's never enough, because there's always more and it's always just out of reach, a rainbow on fire against a black sky, untouchable and so damned perfect it tears at your soul until you bleed but it doesn't make any difference because your blood is on fire, too, and you just keep burning."

Twisting, burning, caught between heaven and hell, hearing Nevada's dark voice and fiery words, Eden fought for the embrace, for the fulfillment she knew blazed just beyond her reach. Nevada bent down to her, holding her motionless while he caught her mouth with his own. She drank his wild hunger, matched it, demanded more and yet more of him until he drove into her, pinning her beneath him, grinding against her as though he would become a part of her or die.

Impaled on ecstasy, consumed by wildfire, Eden would have screamed but she had no breath, no voice, no being. She felt Nevada shuddering beneath rapture's savage blows, heard him cry out as though in torment, but she could not help him for she was him and he was her and together they were the rainbow stretched between heaven and hell, burning.

When the searing fire finally released Eden, she lay spent beneath Nevada, stunned by the passion that had consumed both of them, feeling their bodies fight for breath, for reality. When their breathing finally slowed, Nevada eased himself from Eden's body, caught her face between his hands and looked down into the many colors of her dazed hazel eyes.

"All the colors of life," Nevada whispered, brushing Eden's lips with his own.

As one person, they felt his heartbeat deepen as he quickened against her body once more.

"Nevada?" Eden whispered.

"I can't stop it. I don't even want to try. It's as new to me as it is to you. Fairy-tale girl, all sweet golden fire," he whispered. "Burn with me, fairy-tale girl."

Gently Nevada joined his mouth with Eden's, caressing her sweetly, drinking her with the slow, shared rhythms of remembered hunger and release. The kiss was like his heartbeat, deep and unhurried, certain. Urgency was a distant echo, pleasure a shimmering companion, and their breath whispered as softly as flames in the hearth.

The kiss ended as gently as it had begun, drawing a murmured protest from Eden, for she didn't want it to end. Nevada's lips brushed hers once more, stilling her with a gentle caress that promised things he had no words to say, only a certainty whispering deep inside him, shimmering with pleasures as yet untouched, unknown, unnamed, waiting for them, ecstasy burning as softly as his kisses.

The brush of Nevada's lips closed Eden's eyelids. She sighed as the moist tip of his tongue traced her eyelashes, her hairline, her temples, and his breath caressed her sensitive skin. His words sank gently into her as his teeth and tongue caressed her earlobes, the soft line of her neck, the hollow of her throat, tasting her, sipping her, discovering her. His mouth moved slowly from her shoulders to her fingertips, her breasts, her belly, then down her long legs to the soles of her feet.

Nevada was a warmth moving over Eden, his caresses telling her that she was more beautiful than life, more perfect than fire. The velvet warmth of his tongue was heightened by tiny bites so gentle they made her softly moan. When he knelt between her legs, touched her, cherished her, she wept and gave him what he asked for, opening for him like a flower. He whispered her name and her beauty against her skin, asking for yet another gift, and she gave him that, too, softly bathing him in her fire.

With a gentleness that made Eden tremble, Nevada kissed her, slid his hands beneath her knees and slowly raised her legs, moving them apart with soft pressures and whispered words. Then he lifted his head and looked into Eden's eyes, asking that she trust him in this as she had trusted him in so much already.

The contrast between the heavenly gentleness of Nevada's hands and the shadowy hell in his eyes tore at Eden's heart. She trembled and gave her body to his keeping, heard her name wrapped in the dark velvet of his voice as he gently curled her legs back upon her, leaving nothing secret from him.

There was no embarrassment in Eden this time when Nevada looked at her, kissed her once, twice, and then brought himself to her undefended gate, watching the union as he pressed into her. The taking was so gentle, so slow, his eyes so black, so wild, that Eden unraveled in shivering ecstasy. She saw her undoing echoed in the shudder that rippled through Nevada, but his slow claiming of her softness did not speed up in the least. He took Eden the way dawn takes the night, moment by moment, breath by breath, leaving nothing unclaimed, nothing hidden.

And when he filled her, all of her, sealing their bodies while she watched, she softly moaned at the completion. Tiny convulsions stole through her to him as she shimmered and burst soundlessly into fire. He rocked slowly against her, his movements as gentle and overwhelming as her body unraveling, bathing him in soft flames, rocking, rocking, and she wept and still ecstasy came to her, repeatedly, and each time the gentle rocking, rocking of Nevada's body breathed life into her once more.

And still he rocked gently, filling her, bathing in her fire as they gave themselves to one another in secret molten pulses, burning away the world, leaving only their interlocked bodies and an incandescent ecstasy that had no ending, only beginnings, renewing and consuming and burning until finally they fell asleep, still intimately joined, their interlocked bodies gleaming in the firelight.

Yet even in sleep, Eden wept, for she had seen the darkness in Nevada's eyes and knew she would wake alone.

12

Baby found Nevada's tracks at the base of the ridge that overlooked the cougar's den. The realization that Nevada had been so close to Eden and hadn't so much as said hello drove black splinters of pain into her. Even as Eden looked frantically around, hoping to find Nevada, she knew it would be futile. If he had wanted to talk to her, he would have. He hadn't. He had been very careful not to alert her to his presence, avoiding the keen edge of Baby's senses.

Eden looked at Nevada's tracks and fought not to cry out with loneliness. It had been two weeks since Nevada had come in from one kind of storm, only to create another in the cabin's firelit intimacy. The memories of being joined with Nevada haunted Eden, bringing tears to her eyes even as her body shivered with remembered ecstasy. Blindly she looked at the indentations Nevada's boots had left in the newly fertile earth, then tilted her head back and called into the wind.

"Nevada! Nevada, can't you hear me? I love you!"

Nothing answered. Nothing would. Nevada was gone.

For the first time Eden admitted to herself that her warrior would not come to her again. Her love had not been able to heal Nevada. Even worse, her repeated offerings of love had undermined the peace of mind he had won at such terrible cost in the burned-out villages of Afghanistan.

The real world is a place where all you can do with your prayers and medicine and rage is hold the babies until they die and then bury them and walk away, just walk away, because any man who cares for anything enough to be hurt by its loss is a fool.

Nevada had taken his emotions, locked them up and walked away, forgetting even the existence of a key.

It had worked. Nevada had survived where other men had died. He had stayed sane where other men had gone mad. He had kept control of himself where other men had become savages.

Then Eden had come to the dark warrior, offering love to heal him, offering herself in ways he couldn't refuse, stripping him of the control that was all that had kept him whole.

I'd give my soul not to want you, Eden.

Yet even when cornered, torn apart, wild with the pain of Eden's temptation, even then Nevada had not turned on her, had not defended himself against her with his superior strength and savage skill. Instead, he had given her ecstasy.

In return, she had given him a new taste of old agony. She would die remembering the wild darkness in his eyes and the extraordinary gentleness of his hands.

"Warrior," Eden whispered, trembling, "I'm sorry. I didn't know what I was doing to you. I didn't think what the cost would be if I couldn't heal you."

Eden heard her own words and for the first time understood her own naive arrogance—she had thought herself capable of healing a man she couldn't even make smile. As the instant of understanding came, agony went through her as deeply as ecstasy had, hammer blows of pain twisting through her mind and body, driving her to her knees. With a low sound she bent her head and held on to herself.

The pain, Nevada. My God, the pain.

I would give my soul . . .

After a long time Eden straightened and slowly stood up. Despite the tears that would not stop falling, she walked back to the cabin. There was no reason to stay there any longer, no excuse. Her preliminary survey was complete, her notes were in order, everything was ready to be handed over to others who would decide whether to continue the research at Wildfire Canyon.

She should have left a week ago, but she had stayed on, making excuses about unfinished work, watching the horizon, hoping and praying and hungering for the man she loved. Now nothing remained but to take the advice of the warrior who knew how to survive.

Walk away, just walk away.

Eden began packing up her belongings and stowing them in the truck. Baby watched her with total alertness, yellow eyes intent, sensing that something was wrong. Eden spoke to him quietly from time to time, but never slowed the pace of her movements until the cabin lay empty again, no trace of her presence but the ashes cold in the hearth.

Without a backward look, Eden drove away from Wildfire Canyon, never hesitating until she came to a Y in the dirt track. The left-hand road led to West Fork. The other led to the Rocking M's ranch house.

Eden's mind chose the left-hand fork. Her hands chose the right.

When Eden drove the truck into the ranch house's broad, graveled front drive, there was only one vehicle parked between the house and the barn. She got out of the truck and started to close the door. Baby shot by her in a fluid leap. Once free, he made no attempt to run off. He simply stood and watched her with an unwavering yellow glance that told her he would resist being separated from his mistress. The wolf didn't know what was wrong; he simply knew that something was.

"Heel," Eden said softly.

Baby condensed at her heel like a black shadow.

The sun was almost hot in the ranch yard. Flowers bloomed vividly in the beds that ran along the porch. Their bright colors and soft petals spoke eloquently of winter's surrender to spring.

Eden knocked on the door. A feminine voice answered from the second story.

"Door's open. There's coffee in the kitchen. I'll be with you as soon as I get Logan dried off."

Eden hesitated, then opened the door and walked into the living room. Two playpens stood along the wall beneath a whimsical, hand-carved mobile featuring spurs and branding irons. One playpen was empty. The other held a child dressed in pink who looked about a year old. She was fussing in the manner of a baby who had been awakened too early.

"Sit," Eden said quietly to her wolf. "Stay."

The wolf obeyed, content as long as Eden was within his sight.

Drawn by the little girl's muted fussing, Eden went and stood by the playpen.

"Hello, little angel," she said gently. "I'm sorry I woke you up."

Carolina stopped grumping, looked at the stranger and held her arms out in the confident demand of a well-loved child. Eden bent over and lifted the little girl into her arms. The compact warmth and sleepy resilience of Carolina's body brought back an avalanche of memories of another small person, another compact bundle of warmth, and laughter like a field of poppies in the sun.

Holding Carolina, rocking slowly, humming softly, Eden closed her eyes and prayed that Nevada had given her his child to love.

"I'm Diana Blackthorn," a voice said from behind Eden. "From the looks of that great black beast watching you, you must be Eden Summers."

"His name is Baby," Eden said, turning around and looking at the small woman with the intense blue eyes. "He won't hurt you. But if you're worried, I'll—"

"No problem," Diana interrupted, looking curiously at the motionless wolf. "I've been dying to see Baby ever since Nevada mentioned him."

Eden looked from Carolina to Diana and back again. "She's yours, isn't she," Eden said quietly. "You both have eyes like slices of sapphire."

"Carolina's half mine," Diana agreed, smiling. "Thanks for soothing her. Once she gets going, she's hard to stop. She has the deep-running passion of a Blackthorn."

Eden couldn't conceal the bittersweet shaft of pain lancing through her at Diana's words, but all she said was "Is Luke MacKenzie here?"

"No. He and Carla won't be back until dinner. Mariah and Cash won't be here at all. They've moved into Cortez until the twins are born."

"Is your husband Tennessee Blackthorn, the Rocking M's ramrod?"

"Yes, but he's out working the lease lands on the other side of MacKenzie Ridge. He won't be back until well after sundown. But Nevada should be back within the hour. Perhaps he could help you?"

Eden closed her eyes for an instant, then shook her head very slowly and smoothed her cheek against Carolina's shiny black hair.

"Here," Diana said, looking at Eden's pale face and drawn mouth, "let me take Carolina. She's getting heavier every day. Pretty soon we'll need a crane to lift her."

Reluctantly Eden gave the sleeping child back, shifting Carolina's limp weight with an expertise that hadn't faded in the years since Aurora had died.

"You know how to handle babies," Diana said, bending over and tucking Carolina beneath a fluffy quilt in the playpen. "Do you have children of your own?"

"No, but years ago I had a younger sister. She was just Carolina's size. . . ."

Something in Eden's voice caught at Diana's emotions. She turned and saw the sadness in Eden's eyes.

"Would you pass a message along to Luke MacKenzie?" Eden asked, looking away.

"Of course."

"I've finished the preliminary survey of the cougars in and around Wildfire Canyon. There are two full-time resident cats. One is a mother with three cubs. The other is a young male. I've found absolutely no indication that the cougars are feeding on anything but natural prey."

Diana let out a long sigh and smiled. "That's good news. The Rocking M women really didn't want our men to have to hunt down those cougars. The men weren't happy about the prospect, either, but they would have done it to protect the calves."

Eden felt cold at the thought of Nevada having to kill the mama cougar. Nevada had known too much of death and violence, not enough of love and life.

"I'm glad the mama cougar lives on Rocking M land," Eden said after a moment. "She'll be safe here."

"God, yes. Nevada watches over her like a mother hen. I've been trying to get him to take me to see the cubs, but he's worried about disturbing her before the cubs are old enough to leave the den."

"She's a good mother," Eden said. "All three of her cubs are lively and strong. When she calls to them, she makes the most beautiful fluting sounds...."

Eden closed her eyes and touched the golden chain and the tiny ring lying in the hollow of her throat.

"You look tired, and it's a long way from here to anywhere else," Diana said. "Why don't you stay for dinner and then overnight? Luke and Ten would love to talk to you about the Rocking M's cats."

"Nevada can answer their questions."

"Thanks," Diana said dryly, "but I'd just as soon Ten didn't take on his brother right now. Carla feels the same way about Luke. Nevada never was an outgoing kind of man, but in the past few weeks he's set new records. He's shut down, sealed up, and his eyes are enough to give your wolf pause. Frankly, Ten and I were kind of hoping you would show up here. Anyone else who tries to reach Nevada will get their head handed to them."

Slowly Eden shook her head.

"Don't misunderstand me," Diana said quickly, touching Eden's arm. "Nevada is a good man. A woman wouldn't have to worry about her safety with him. He would never hurt you physically. He's capable of great gentleness, too. You should see him with Carla's new baby. It's enough to make me cry."

"I know," Eden whispered.

"Then why won't you stay and talk to him?"

"Because he doesn't want to talk to me."

There was no mistaking the pain in Eden's voice, in her expression, in the fine trembling of her fin-

gers as she reached up and unfastened the gold
chain from around her neck. Carefully she looped
the chain on the curve of the Rocking M brand. The
gold glistened like sunlight caught in the mobile's
changing lines.

"Eden?"

"Tell Luke that the university will send him a
copy of my report, including photographs of the
cougars' tracks and sketches of the boundaries of
their territories," Eden said, her voice husky. "And
tell him thank-you from the bottom of my heart.
Too many ranchers simply would have killed the
cats out of suspicion and mistrust and ignorance."

Eden turned and walked quickly to the door. At
a single small movement of her hand, Baby rose.
With the silence of smoke, the wolf followed Eden
outdoors. Behind them the chain and its tiny
braided gold ring shimmered and shone above the
sleeping Blackthorn child.

When Nevada came in the front door of the
ranch house, his first stop was always the playpens. They were empty, which meant that the
"Rocking M Monsters" were getting their bedtime
baths. Disappointed at having missed a chance to
play with Carolina and Logan, Nevada took off his
black Stetson, snapped it against his thigh, and
tugged the hat back into place on his head.

"Need any help?" Nevada called up the stairs.

"So far, so good," Carla called back. "Coffee's ready in the kitchen."

Nevada poured himself a mug of coffee and went back to the living room, bothered by something he couldn't name. Eyes narrowed, he looked around while the squeals of a child splashing enthusiastically in the bath drifted down the stairs. Though nothing seemed obviously out of place in the living room, something kept nagging at Nevada just beneath the threshold of conscious thought, telling him that all was *not* as it seemed.

Stirred by the passage of Nevada's restless body, the mobiles moved. A shimmer of gold caught his eye. He turned and walked closer. An instant later he recognized the chain and the tiny braided ring he had last seen nestled in the hollow of Eden's throat. Nevada's breath stopped as his heart contracted in his chest.

I wear Aurora's ring to remind myself that love is never wasted, never futile.

Shards of past conversations sliced through him, making him bleed with a pain he had vowed never to feel.

I love you, Nevada.

That's what I was afraid you were telling your-self. Fairy tales. You can't accept that all there is between us is sex. Pure and simple and hot as hell.

With great care Nevada freed the delicate chain from the mobile.

I'm worlds too hard for you, but I want you until my hands shake.

Now I know what life tastes like.

Eden's fingertips brushing him, her husky voice whispering, words burning into his soul and the tiny ring gleaming as light caressed the intertwined strands of gold.

I'm not offering you love and happily ever after. I can't be what you want me to be.

Hazel eyes luminous, alive with all the colors of life, watching him, loving him.

Love is never wasted. Never. But it can hurt like nothing else on earth.

Heaven and hell and the rainbow burning between.

I would sell my soul not to want you.

Fairy-tale girl, all laughter and golden light.

But no longer.

He had stripped her of laughter as surely as he had stripped her of innocence. She had loved him; he had denied that love was possible. He had left her without a word of hope...and now she no longer wore the chain and its tiny gold ring.

She hadn't been able to teach him to believe in love, but he had been able to teach her to believe in despair.

Nevada made the low sound of a man who has just taken a body blow. He hadn't meant to destroy anything at all, much less something as rare and beautiful as Eden. Yet he had destroyed just the same. The proof was lying in his hand, a dead child's ring and a living woman's endless loss.

For a long time Nevada stood motionless, staring into space, seeing nothing, not even his own tears.

The long wind blew, sweeping down out of the distant mountains, bringing restlessness to the mixed evergreen forest. A river ran pale with glacial melt, brawling through the wide, flat valley down to the sea. Everywhere there was the subdued frenzy of life that has only a short growing season and a whole new generation to raise.

Eden sat in the small log cabin that had been her parents' first Alaskan home and now was hers. Although the early June day was vibrant with sunlight and wind, she wasn't out searching for lynx across the fertile green land. The changes in her body had made her sleepy, slightly nauseated, lacking any ambition other than to sit in the sun and remind herself that tears were wasted. If she could have gone back and lived again the weeks in Colorado, she would have changed nothing that was within her power to change.

And if Eden were haunted by memories of a warrior's unsmiling green eyes and gentle, passionate hands, then so be it. She would not change that, either. Nevada had given her more of beauty and ecstasy than she had ever dreamed of having. The fact that the pain of her loss was greater, too, than she had imagined possible, was something she would just have to live through as she had lived through the loss of Aurora, enduring until the bitter and the sweet were inextricably mixed, each defining and refining the other until they became a seamless, beautiful whole.

Baby sat near Eden's feet, looking through the screen door toward the uninhabited land. His long black ears were erect, his narrow muzzle tipped into the cool rush of air, his yellow eyes gleaming.

Without warning he came to his feet in a lithe rush, drank the wind, and tipped back his head in a howl. The eerie, primal sound froze Eden. She heard that particular howl from Baby only when she returned to him after a long absence. But she hadn't been absent. Her body had been present all the time, if not her heart and mind.

Perhaps Mark had returned early from his stint in the oil fields.

Eden sighed and stood up. As she opened the screen door, a man stepped from the willows sheltering the path to the cabin. His shoulders were wide and his walk was as easy as that of a cougar prowling. The world tipped and spun dizzily, forcing Eden to hang on to the door frame or fall.

It can't be. Nevada.

Baby leaped through the open door and hit the ground running and yapping, nearly walking on the sky in delight. Nevada caught the wolf in midleap, spun around, and sent Baby flying off in another direction. The wolf turned nimbly and launched himself at the man again in a game that the two of them had created in a land thousands of miles distant.

Numbly Eden watched wolf and warrior play, wondering if she were dreaming . . . or if she had simply gone mad.

When the first exuberance of Baby's greeting was quenched, Nevada looked toward the cabin door. A single glance at Eden's blank face told him that the mistress wasn't nearly as happy to see him as her wolf had been.

"Hello, Eden. You look . . ."

Nevada's voice died. He had no words to describe how Eden looked to him. Nor could he describe his hunger to hold her warmth and laughter within his arms once more.

"How did you find me?" she asked finally.

"It took some doing. I had to lean on some folks at the university pretty hard before they gave me any help."

Nevada's light green eyes searched Eden's face, noting each sign of change, but most of all he saw the darkness of her eyes, a darkness she tried to conceal by looking away.

"Don't," he said softly.

"What?"

"Don't look away from me."

"I can't—I—seeing you—"

Eden laced her fingers together and looked at Nevada and felt as though she were being torn apart.

I'd give my soul not to want you.

She knew how Nevada felt, now. Too late.

She tried to take a deep, steadying breath, but no matter how much air she took in, it wasn't enough. The world was spinning too quickly, she was off balance, no center, nothing stable, nothing but the longing for Nevada that would not end.

"Eden!"

Nevada caught Eden as her knees gave away, carried her into the cabin and set her gently on the bed. The pallor of her skin made him want to cry out in protest. Her lashes stirred, then opened to reveal eyes that were darker than he remembered. She started to sit up.

"No," he said, catching Eden's shoulders gently, pressing her back into the bed, brushing his lips over her forehead, her cheek. "Just lie still, fairy-tale girl."

Nevada's glance went over Eden like hands, noting everything. His nostrils flared, drinking in the subtle change in her scent. His whole body went still. He lifted his head and looked into her eyes.

"You're pregnant," he said flatly. "I knew it. Damn those university bureaucrats! I should have been here weeks ago!" He cursed once, savagely. "Is everything all right?"

"Yes."

"Bull. You fainted."

"Shock, not pregnancy." Eden closed her eyes, unable to bear Nevada's scrutiny. "I never expected to see you again. It was like having someone come back from the dead."

"Why didn't you tell me?"

"That I'm pregnant?"

Nevada nodded curtly.

"And make you feel even more trapped than you did in Wildfire Canyon?" Eden shook her head and opened her eyes. "I can't bear watching your pain. I can't heal it. I can only make it worse. I won't do that, Nevada." Not wanting to, unable to stop herself, she lifted her hand and touched the coarse silk of his beard. "Don't worry, warrior. I'll be a good mother to our child."

"But you don't think I'll be good father."

"In every way but one, you would be a marvelous father."

Nevada waited, watching Eden with hooded eyes.

"Children need love," she whispered. "You don't believe in it."

"Neither do you, now. I took that from you as surely as I took your innocence."

Eden stared at Nevada. "What do you mean?"

He reached into his shirt pocket and brought out a golden chain and tiny braided ring.

"You told me that you wore this to remind you that love was never wasted, never futile. *And then you left it behind.*"

"I didn't need Aurora's ring anymore. My reminder was alive within me. Your baby, Nevada. My baby. Our baby. A child of the love you don't believe in. But I understand why, now. If you allowed yourself to feel emotion, you would be vulnerable again. Your emotions run strong and hard and so very deep. Your ability to feel could destroy you. It nearly did. So you walked away from feeling, from emotion, from love."

"Eden, I..." Nevada's throat closed.

She smiled sadly. "It's all right, warrior. If I weren't pregnant, I would have done the same thing you did. Walked away from feeling, shed my pain like a snake shedding skin, and walked away, just walked away. Then I held Carolina and remembered little Aurora's laughter and I prayed that I was pregnant. And I am. Thank you for that, Nevada. Thank you for allowing your control to slip that much."

Eden's husky voice made Nevada's throat close around emotions he no longer could deny. Silently he bent down and fastened the gold chain around Eden's neck once more. The metal was warm from his body, almost weightless. He kissed the tiny gold ring where it lay in the soft hollow of her throat, then gathered Eden close and held her, simply held her, fighting for the self-control that always slipped away when he was close to Eden.

"Do you want to live here or on the Rocking M after we're married?" Nevada asked without lifting his face from the warm curve of Eden's neck.

The subtle rasp in his voice was like a cat's tongue licking over Eden's nerves. The temptation he offered was dizzying, almost overwhelming.

"No," she breathed.

"Then where?"

"No. Just no."

"Why?"

"Don't. Please, don't. If I weren't pregnant, you wouldn't be talking about marriage."

"Are you sure of that?" Nevada asked softly.

"I'm sure I can't bear to watch your eyes turn bleaker each time we make love," Eden said with desperate calm. "I'm sure I can't bear being something you don't want yet can't refuse." She closed her eyes but couldn't prevent her tears from falling as she whispered, "I can't heal you but I can set you free. Walk away, warrior, just walk away."

Eden felt Nevada stir, sitting up, moving away from her. It was what she knew must be, yet even knowing it she had to bite back a cry of pain.

The feel of Nevada's lips against Eden's left hand was like a soft brand burning her. She made a tiny sound of protest, but couldn't free her hand. Something smooth and warm slid over her third finger.

"Open your eyes," Nevada said, brushing away Eden's tears with his kisses.

When Eden opened her eyes she saw gold gleaming on her ring finger, a circle of braided metal that was exactly like the tiny ring lying in the hollow of her throat. Silently Nevada held out his left hand. On his hard palm a third ring gleamed, golden braids intertwined.

"If you believe I can love," he said, "put the ring on me."

Eden looked into his eyes for a long moment, remembering the instant when she had caught his wrist in the bar and seen both the darkness and the light that was Nevada. Slowly she picked up the golden ring, kissed it and slid it onto his finger, whispering her love against his palm. Nevada kissed her ring in return, lifted his head, and looked into the eyes that saw so deeply into him, accepting him for what he was, loving him despite the darkness he had known.

Her love was like stepping into the sun, a blazing joy transforming him as surely as pain once had.

"Nevada . . . ?"

Eden's breath stopped, for she had seen nothing more beautiful than her dark warrior's smile, a smile to make angels weep. With trembling fingers she touched Nevada's lips. His hard and gentle hands framed her face, holding her, seeing the reflection of his newfound freedom in her radiant hazel eyes.

"You are my life, my soul, everything I wanted and feared I would never have," Nevada whispered, bending down to Eden. "Fairy-tale girl, I love you."

Bestselling Author

Jasmine Cresswell

**May 1995 brings you face-to-face with her
latest thrilling adventure**

Desires & Deceptions

Will the real Claire Campbell please stand up?
Missing for over seven years, Claire's family has
only one year left to declare her legally dead and
claim her substantial fortune—that is, until a woman
appears on the scene alleging to be the missing
heiress. Will DNA testing solve the dilemma? Do
old family secrets still have the power to decide
who lives and dies, suffers or prospers, loves or
hates? Only Claire knows for sure.

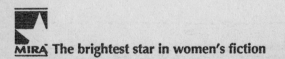

Take 3 of "The Best of the Best™" Novels FREE

Plus get a FREE surprise gift!

Special Limited-time Offer

Mail to The Best of the Best™

> 3010 Walden Avenue
> P.O. Box 1867
> Buffalo, N.Y. 14269-1867

YES! Please send me 3 free novels and my free surprise gift. Then send me 3 of "The Best of the Best™" novels each month. I'll receive the best books by the world's hottest romance authors. Bill me at the low price of $3.74 each plus 25¢ delivery and applicable sales tax, if any.* That's the complete price and a savings of over 10% off the cover prices—quite a bargain! I understand that accepting the books and gift places me under no obligation ever to buy any books. I can always return a shipment and cancel at any time. Even if I never buy another book from Harlequin, the 3 free books and the surprise gift are mine to keep forever.

183 BPA ANV9

Name	(PLEASE PRINT)	
Address	Apt. No.	
City	State	Zip

This offer is limited to one order per household and not valid to current subscribers.
*Terms and prices are subject to change without notice. Sales tax applicable in N.Y.
All orders subject to approval.

UBOB-295

©1990 Harlequin Enterprises Limited

Over 10 million books in print!

Diana Palmer

An independent woman meets a determined
man this April in

Lady Love

Men had always wanted Merlyn Forrest for her
money, until she met handsome, serious and
dangerously seductive Cameron Thorpe. He
wasn't after her money, but he did want her
body—and her soul. She was too independent
to let any man control her life, but if he really
wanted her, he would have to play by her
rules...or not play at all.

Seduction most dangerous.

Award-winning romance author

LINDA HOWARD

This April, face some unexpected complications in

The Cutting Edge

Brett Rutland was an expert at catching corporate
thieves with cold, unerring precision. Then
he met beautiful and desirable executive
Tessa Conway. Life was perfect...until the day
Brett identified the embezzler within Tessa's
company.

Could their love withstand the ultimate challenge?

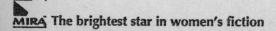

If you're looking for more titles by

ELIZABETH LOWELL

don't miss this chance to order these stories by
one of MIRA's most distinguished authors: